400 FUNNY G

© 2005 Teora USA LLC
2 Wisconsin Circle, Suite 870
Chevy Chase, MD 20815, USA
for the English version.
Translated by Adriana Badescu and Gina Ivasuc
500 Jeux amusants
© Editions CARAMEL S.A.
Otto de Mentockplein 19
1853 Strombeek-Bever - Belgium

#056

ISBN 1-59496-008-9

Printed in Romania

10 9 8 7 6 5 4 3 2 1

400 FUNNY GAMES

for smart kids

Teora

1. Which vine must Tarzan use to get out of the jungle?

2. Which of these animals don't live in the forest?

3. Find the three differences.

4. Find these details in the drawings.

5. Can you do these calculations?

28 − 6 = ...

14 ÷ 7 = ...

2 × 5 = ...

5 − 3 = ...

7 + 2 = ...

3 × 4 = ...

4

6. Join the numbers in the correct order in these two drawings.

Color the drawings.

5

7. Draw the haircuts as indicated.

short

long

curly

8. Find the five differences in the picture with the Mexican.

10. Add the numbers to obtain 40. Start with 0.

9. Find the three differences in the pictures illustrating a boy with a kite.

1	40	5	3	5	1	2		1	2	1	40		1	3		4
2	6	3	2	6	40		4	2	2	3	5	2	3	2	2		3
5	2	3	2	2			3	0		3	2	4	1	5	4	2	1
3	1	2	6	5	4	1	2		6	3	2	5	3	2	1	
4	2		4	3	2	5	6	3	5	2	1	5		1	1	3	5
	2	40	1	2	4	2	1	4		6	4		2	40		4

11. What are these monsters called?

12. Discover the shortest way to get out of the maze while avoiding the wild animal.

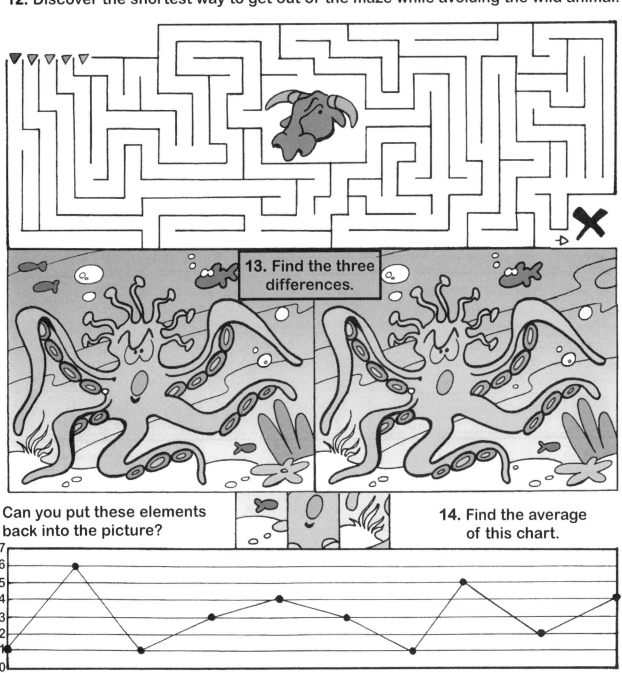

13. Find the three differences.

Can you put these elements back into the picture?

14. Find the average of this chart.

15. Draw the following trees:

apple tree   palm tree   pine

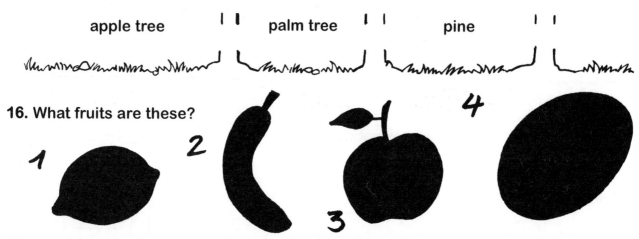

16. What fruits are these?

1   *2*   *3*   *4*

17. **Across:** 1. of or like an abyss; unfathomable 6. an item that combines with others to form a set 7. any of the Scandinavian seafaring peoples who raided and settled in much of NW Europe between the 8th and 11th centuries. 9. in dates: Anno Domini (Latin), in the year of our Lord, used together with a figure to indicate a specified number of years after that in which Christ was once thought to have been born (abbr.) 11. a prefix meaning new, recent 13. stylishness; elegance 15. substance found in coffee 16. a tiny supernatural being with a human form, with a tendency to play tricks

Down: 2. a set of words, short poem to be sung, usually with accompanying music 3. a green plant with large edible leaves used in salads 4. a payment made before it is due 5. expressing agreement or approval; all right; 6. United Nations International Children & Emergency Fund (abbr.) 8. the highest standard of behavior, perfection, beauty 10. of high quality; excellent; splendid 12. away; at or to a distance 14. a casual form of greeting

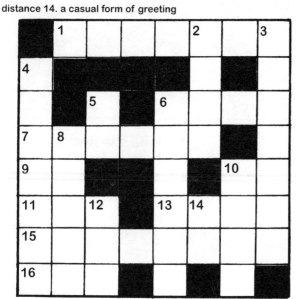

18. Which is the closest and which is the most remote balloon, knowing that they are the same size.

8

19. Find the route from 1 to 20. Two consecutive figures must be next to each other.

1	2	5	6	7	8	9	10
2	3	4	5	6	7	8	11
5	4	5	6	7	8	9	12
6	7	10	11	12	9	10	13
7	8	9	12	11	10	11	12
8	13	14	13	16	17	18	13
9	12	15	14	15	20	19	14
10	11	16	17	16	17	16	15

20. Find the following numbers: 5, 3, 4, 7, 6, 2, 1, 8, 9.

21. Look for the drawing below in the opposite image.

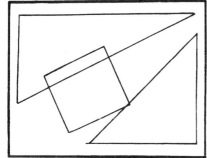

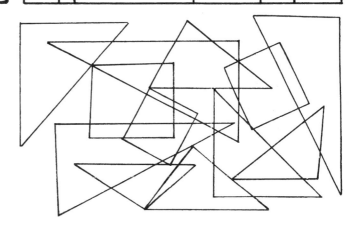

22. Try to make the pattern "OXO" every time you write an X or an O.

O			X		X		O		O
	X	O	X		X				
O						X	X	O	O
	X	X							
			O			O			O
X			X						X
O						O			
	X				X	X			X
O			X	O		O			O

23. Complete these calculations to obtain the precise result.

$$5...5...5...5 = 25$$
$$5...5...5...5 = 30$$
$$5...5...5...5 = 9$$
$$5..5...5..5 = 50$$
$$5...5...5..5 = 75$$
$$5...5...5...5 = 11$$
$$5..5...5...5 = 10$$
$$5..5...5..5 = 120$$
$$5..5..5...5 = 45$$

24. Two of these pictures are identical. Which ones?

25. Two trains are coming from opposite directions and there is only one way to pass each other without accident. One engine and three cars can pass at one time on the A railway track. There is no limit to the number of cars that may pass on track B. How can you solve the problem? One clue: the trains can move forward and backward.

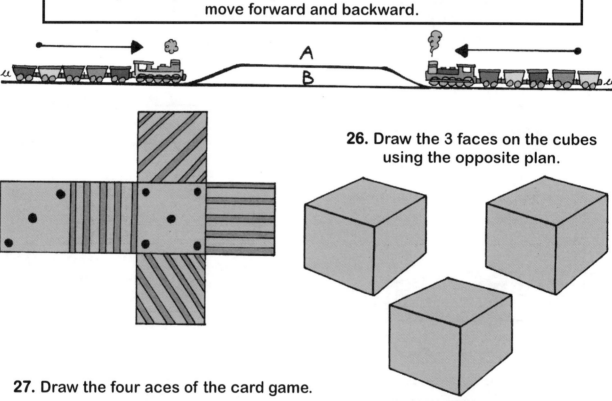

26. Draw the 3 faces on the cubes using the opposite plan.

27. Draw the four aces of the card game.

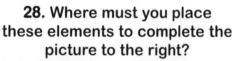

28. Where must you place these elements to complete the picture to the right?

10

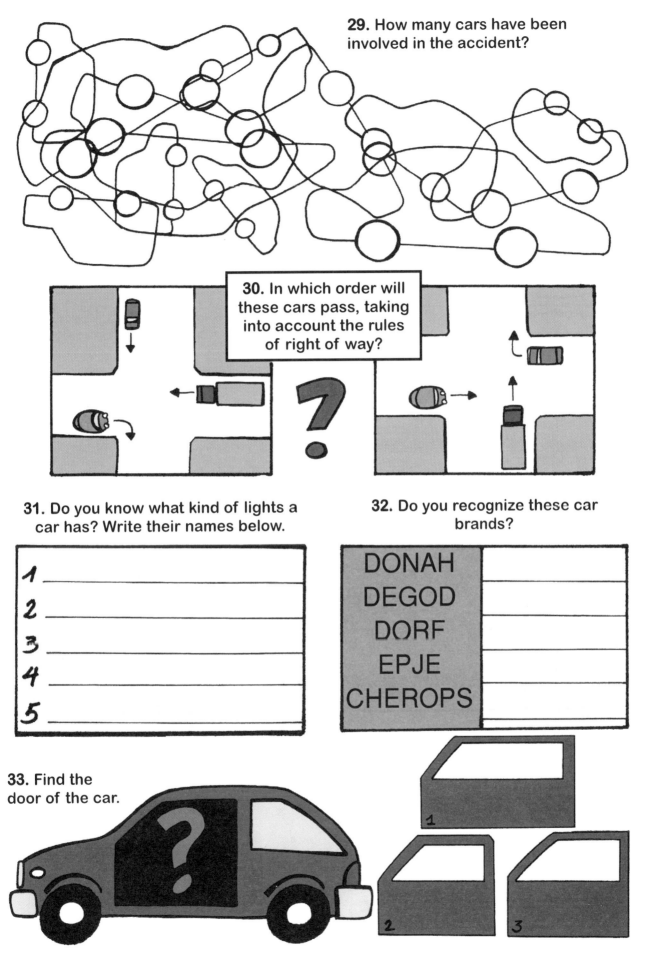

29. How many cars have been involved in the accident?

30. In which order will these cars pass, taking into account the rules of right of way?

31. Do you know what kind of lights a car has? Write their names below.

1 _____
2 _____
3 _____
4 _____
5 _____

32. Do you recognize these car brands?

DONAH	
DEGOD	
DORF	
EPJE	
CHEROPS	

33. Find the door of the car.

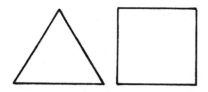

34. Draw the proper shape instead of the question mark, taking into account the other shapes.

9	4	1	3	2	3	4	2
3	10	6	3	4	5	2	9

35. Every time the frog takes a leap the cars advance one box. What number must the frog start from in order to safely cross the road?

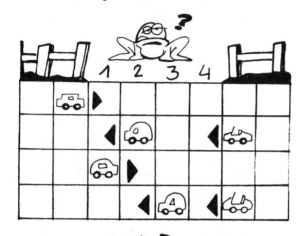

36. Complete the operations using the numbers above. Attention: each number may be used only once.

$$((...+...)-(...+...))+... = 10$$
$$((...÷...)+(...+...))-... = 6$$
$$(...-...-...)+(...×...) = 16$$

37. Finish drawing this nice peacock.

Color the peacock.

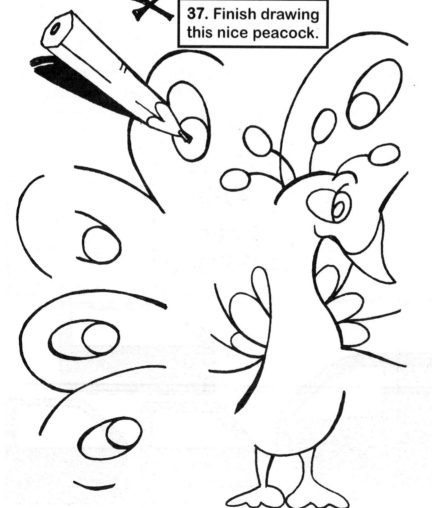

38. Choose one car near the figure 50 and then start adding the numbers on this circuit to 50 without running over the other cars.

39. Color the cars with fog lights.

VVHHHEEE ROOOAAAMM

40. Which wheel must the mechanic fix?

41. Put your pencil on the start line and cover the circuit with your eyes closed.

42. Find the object that has nothing to do with the car race.

43. The navigation program of the robot is broken. Show him the shortest way. Choose from the table on the right and circle the ones you use.

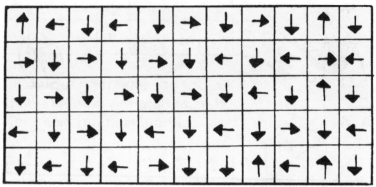

44. Find the identical fragment in the group of four above.

45. Divide this square in eight equal triangles using just four lines.

46. Find the averages of the numbers indicated below.

$$^{10}/_{10} , \quad ^2/_5 , \quad ^4/_{10} , \quad ^3/_{15} =$$

$$^2/_8 , \quad ^3/_4 , \quad ^6/_{12} , \quad ^2/_2 =$$

$$^2/_6 , \quad ^3/_9 , \quad ^4/_6 , \quad ^6/_9 =$$

$$^4/_{16} , \quad ^2/_8 , \quad ^3/_{12} , \quad ^{16}/_{16} =$$

47. Which one is each child's balloon?

49. Complete the math problem as necessary to obtain the result on top of this strength-measuring scale.

48. Find these children's five differences.

51. Find the shortest way to get out of this maze.

50. What is hiding behind these shadows?

15

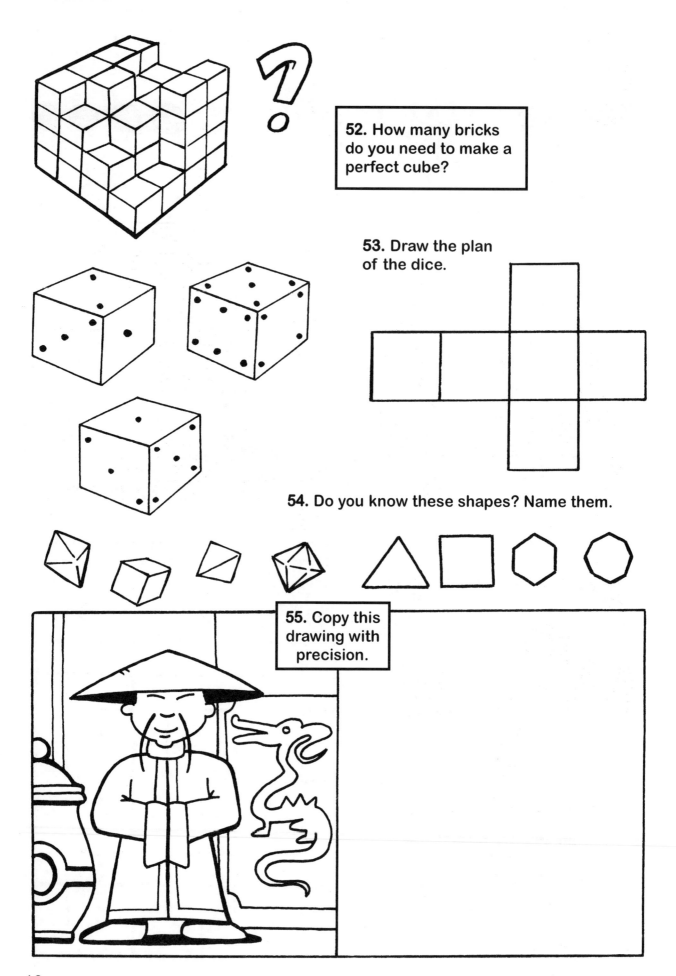

52. How many bricks do you need to make a perfect cube?

53. Draw the plan of the dice.

54. Do you know these shapes? Name them.

55. Copy this drawing with precision.

56. The glazier wonders which windowpane to use. Can you help him?

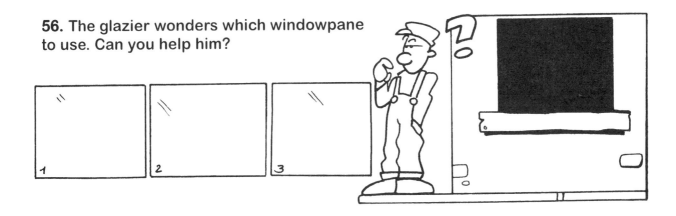

57. Help the architect draw the front and top views of the house.

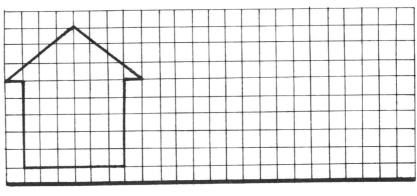

side view   top view   front view

side view   top view   front view

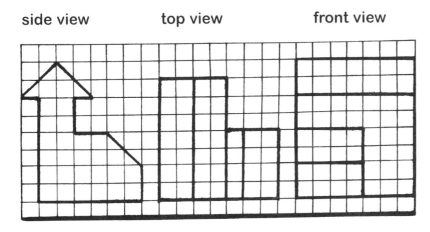

Draw the building following the architect's plans.

58. Replace each letter with its position number in the alphabet and solve the calculation. Think that letters are numbers.

A + B = . .
D × C = . .
Z − Y = . .
Z ÷ B = . .

59. Write the missing numbers.

2	4		8		12
3	5		9		13
2	5		11		17

17

60. Create the longest word using the indicated letters.

A	Y	O
S	R	N
T	M	O

A	T	I
E	R	H
C	T	C

R	E	P
U	E	A
D	T	R

E	H	T
G	O	D
R	O	M

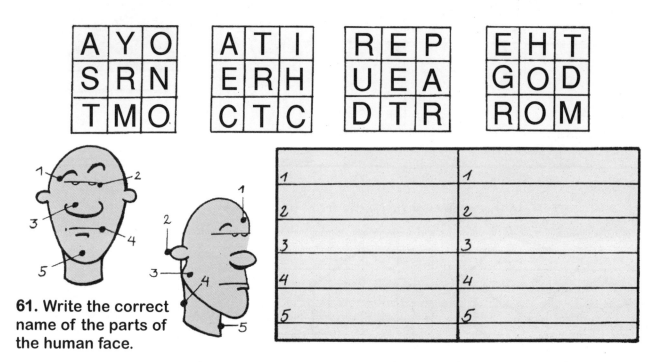

61. Write the correct name of the parts of the human face.

1	1
2	2
3	3
4	4
5	5

62. Find three differences.

63. Fill in the empty boxes so that the results for every row and column are the same.

	6	
	12	
	6	

	3	
	5	
	1	

64. Discover the name of an African city by starting with J and moving like the knight in chess.

J	A	E	U
S	R	O	N
H	N	B	G

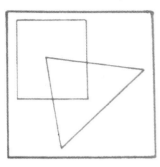

65. Find these shapes in the opposite mess.

66. What do these shadows represent? Which one doesn't belong? Explain your reasons.

67. The king entrusted the key of the palace to Princess Forgetall, who wanted to go into the forest. Once she arrived in the forest, the princess noticed that she had lost the key. Can you find it?

 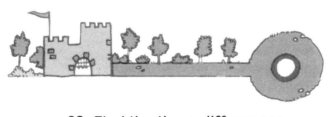 

68. Find the three differences.

69. Write your blood type here.

70. The doctor is absent minded. Help him by showing the following organs: the lungs, the intestines, the tonsils, the stomach, and the liver.

71. Which of these symbols don't represent blood types?

$$D^+, A^-, C^+, O^-$$

72. Two radiographies are identical. Which ones?

73. Which of these instruments don't belong in the surgical kit?

1   2   3   4   5

74. Write the names of these three ways to give medicine.

1 _____
2 _____
3 _____

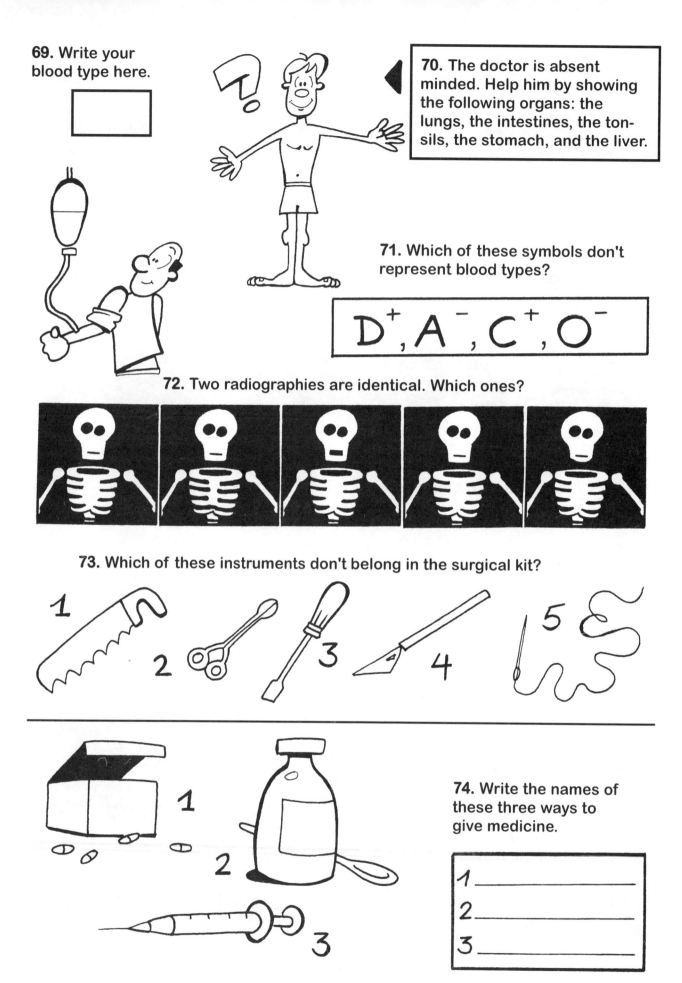

20

75. Get the robot out of the maze.
Each arrow can be used just once.

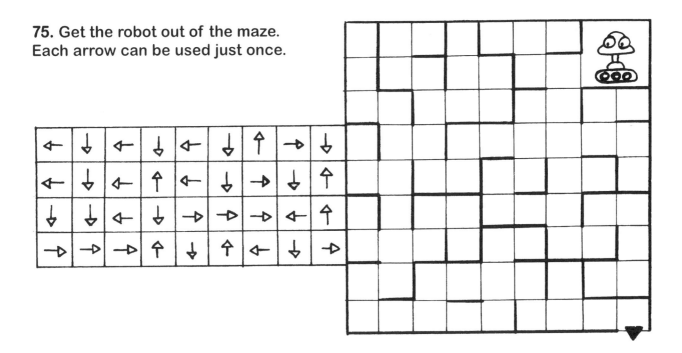

76. Use the chess knight's move
to obtain the given result.

→	1	2	3	1	2	2	4	1	5	2	2	5	4	1	5	3	**35**
→	4	3	1	3	4	2	2	3	2	4	1	4	3	2	3	4	**30**
→	2	2	2	4	5	3	3	1	1	1	3	1	5	1	5	2	**20**
→	3	1	2	5	2	1	3	2	4	4	3	2	2	3	4	1	**25**

77. With which pieces can
you make a square?

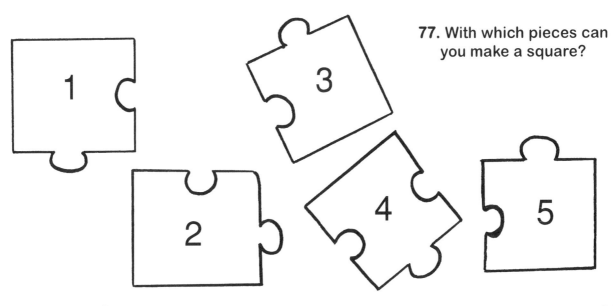

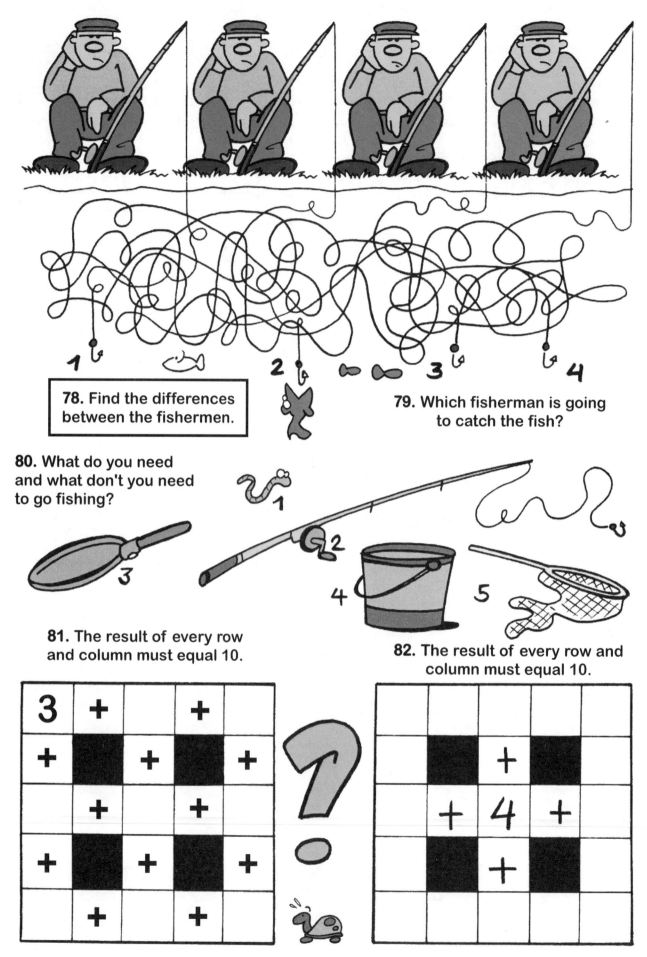

78. Find the differences between the fishermen.

79. Which fisherman is going to catch the fish?

80. What do you need and what don't you need to go fishing?

81. The result of every row and column must equal 10.

82. The result of every row and column must equal 10.

83. From what countries do these foods come?

1 2 3 4

84. How many slices will make a complete pizza?

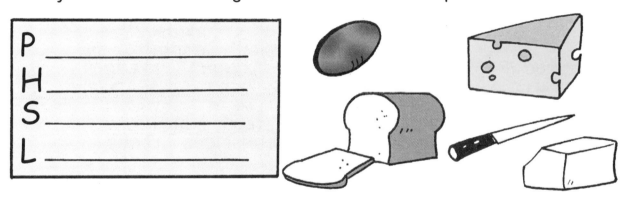

85. Do you know dishes starting with…

P _____
H _____
S _____
L _____

86. Which of these products are milk based?

87. Write your favorite recipe and illustrate it.

23

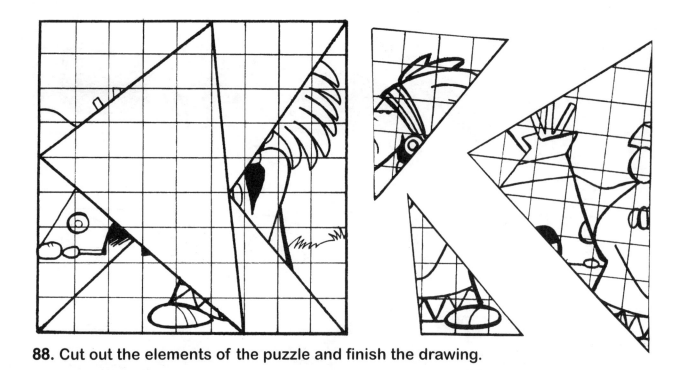

88. Cut out the elements of the puzzle and finish the drawing.

89. Order the following words alphabetically:

HYACINTH RABBIT MEASURE KILO BANANA
PIROUETTE MILLION BOOK WAGON
PIGGY BANK WAX CHERRY PICTURE KIMONO HYENA
LONG BALL MASHED POTATOES MERIT CHATTERING
KILT HYGIENE BAKER SLOWLY MEAN WAPITI
CORKSCREW BALLET INCOMPLETE SQUIRREL
MONTHLY TENT INNOCENT UNCONSCIOUS LENGTH
WATT ORNAMENT PIROGUE
BLONDE LONGITUDE WATER POLO
EMBERS BREEZE TARGET

90. Can you recognize the name of these groups and singers?

NOMADAN
KIPN LOFDY
YLKEI ONGIMUE
MJI SORMNORI
VSLIE REPLESY

91. Do you know their songs?

92. Build a truck using these various pieces.

93. What animals make up this funny animal?

94. Finish the drawing.

95. To what type of vehicles do these wheels and handlebars belong?

1

2

3

4

96. Across: 1. a collection of myths 4. easily agitated 6. unusual; strange; bizarre 7. to perceive (sounds) with the ear 8. any of various toothed cutting tools used especially for cutting wood. 9. an expression of agreement or consent
Down: 1. the range of dishes available in a restaurant 2. violently destructive storms 3. of the color of gold, butter, egg yolk, a lemon 5. prepared and available for use or action 7. in what way; by what means

97. Two of these pictures are identical. Which ones?

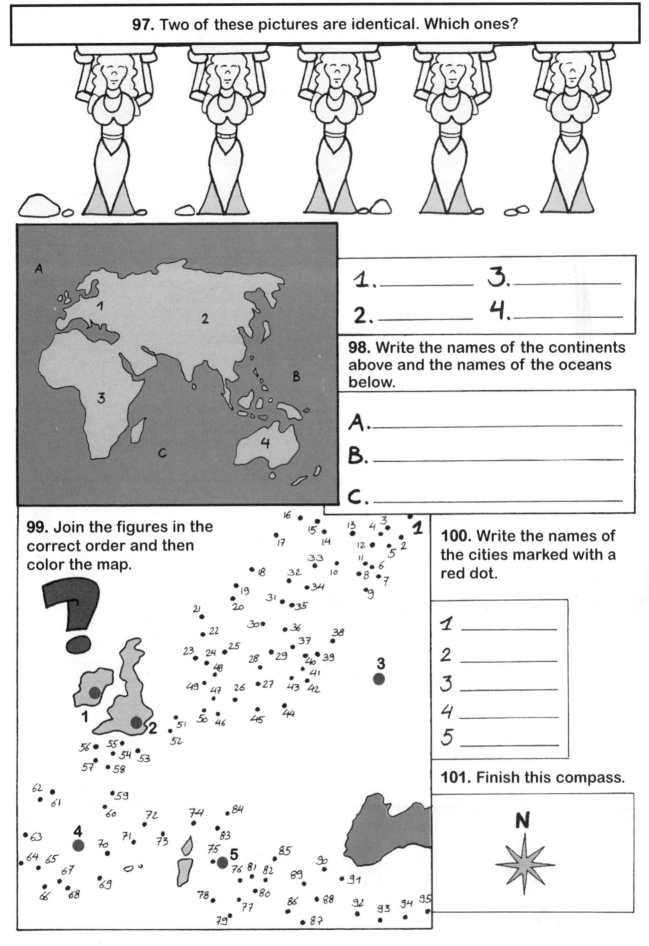

98. Write the names of the continents above and the names of the oceans below.

1. _____   3. _____
2. _____   4. _____

A. _____
B. _____
C. _____

99. Join the figures in the correct order and then color the map.

100. Write the names of the cities marked with a red dot.

1 _____
2 _____
3 _____
4 _____
5 _____

101. Finish this compass.

N

116. Draw the indicated expressions.

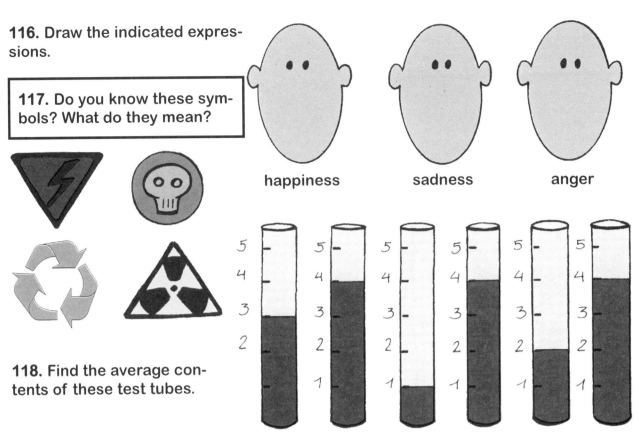

happiness   sadness   anger

117. Do you know these symbols? What do they mean?

118. Find the average contents of these test tubes.

119. Discover the five differences.

31

120. How many of these animals lay eggs? What are their names?

Which of these animals live in Africa?

Take your crayons and color this drawing!

Which of these animals are carnivores?

121. Color this drawing following the code.

- • yellow
- ○ red
- ▢ orange
- △ brown
- ✕ blue

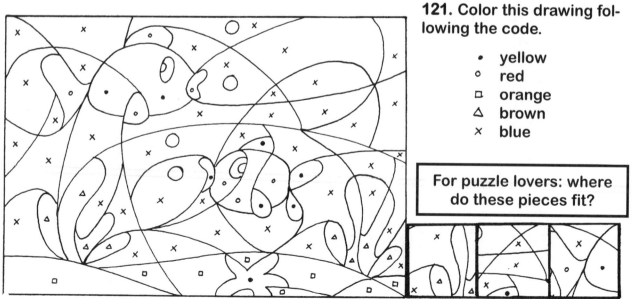

For puzzle lovers: where do these pieces fit?

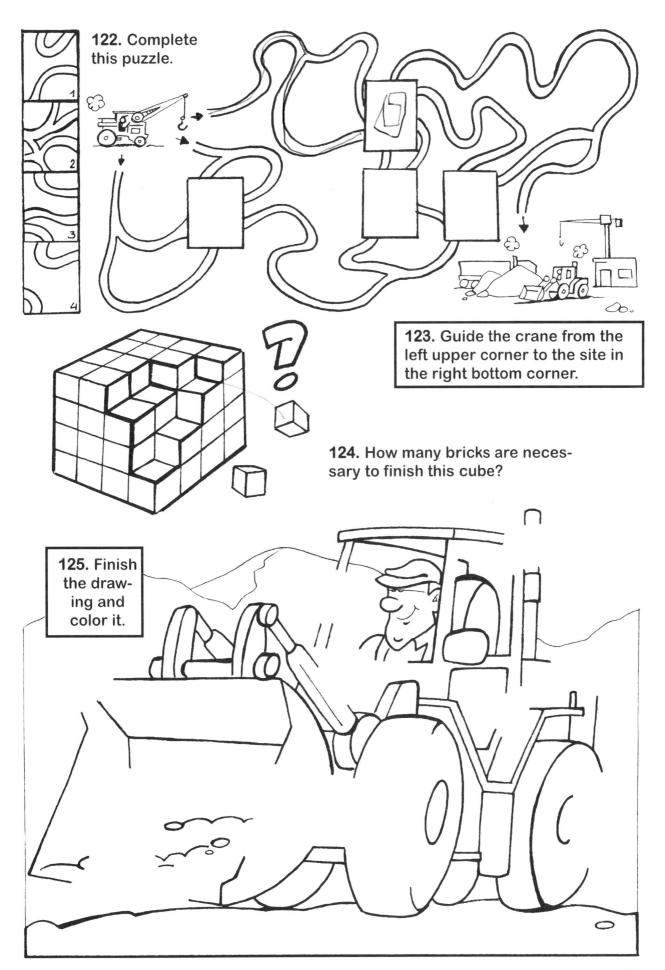

122. Complete this puzzle.

123. Guide the crane from the left upper corner to the site in the right bottom corner.

124. How many bricks are necessary to finish this cube?

125. Finish the drawing and color it.

126. Find the following American presidents:

Across: 1. thirty-second president (1933-1945); first name Franklin
3. thirty-third president (1945-1953); first name Harry 4. first president (1789- 1797); first name George
7. thirty-eighth president (1974-1977); first name Gerald

Down: 1. fortieth president (1981-1989); first name Ronald 2. sixteenth president (1861- 1865); first name Abraham 5. thirty-first president (1929-1933); first name Herbert
6. thirty-seventh president (1969-1974); first name Richard

127. Find the animals hidden in this drawing and color it.

34

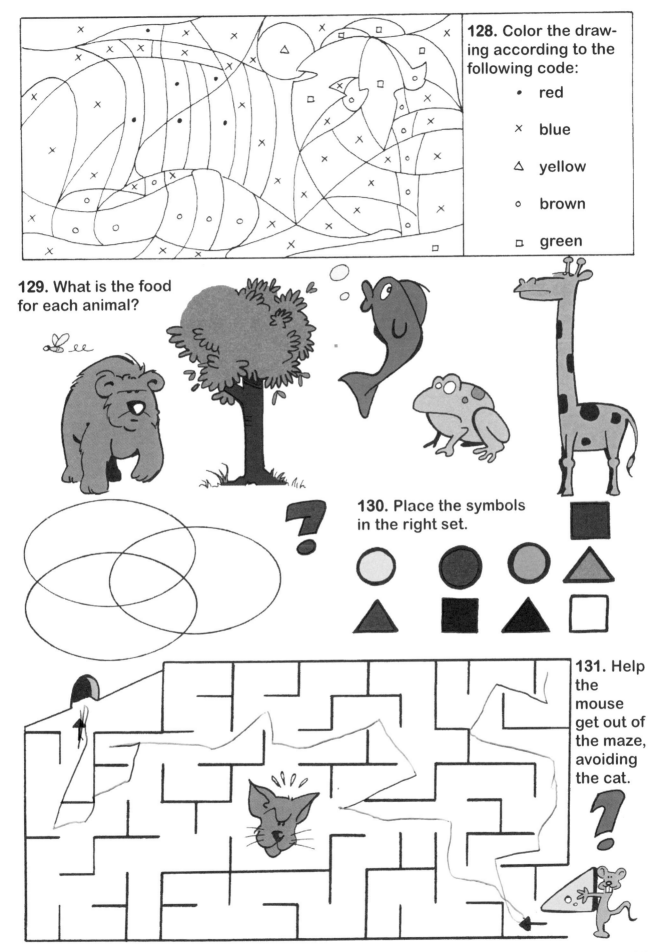

128. Color the drawing according to the following code:

- • red
- × blue
- △ yellow
- ○ brown
- ▢ green

129. What is the food for each animal?

130. Place the symbols in the right set.

131. Help the mouse get out of the maze, avoiding the cat.

132. Find the numbers hidden in this drawing. After that color it.

Where do these pieces fit in the puzzle?

133. These little aliens left us the key to their secret writing. Solve the problems by using the code below.

$1 = \square$

$2 = \bigcirc$

$3 = \square$

$4 = \triangle$

$\triangle + \bigcirc\square - \square =$

$\bigcirc \times \triangle + \bigcirc\square =$

$\square\bigcirc - \triangle - \triangle =$

$\square\square \div \square + \bigcirc =$

$\bigcirc\triangle \div \square\bigcirc + \square =$

134. Help the fly find its way out of the spider's web.

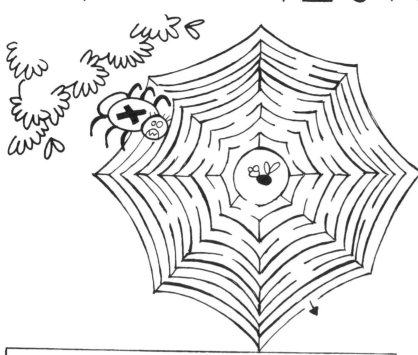

135. Decipher the code and complete the series.

↑ + ⚵ = ..

ⱺ − ♡ = ..

8 × ♡ = ..

∞ ÷ 8 = ..

⚵ + 8 = ..

⚵ ÷ ♡ = ..

ⱺ − ↑ = ..

136. Color the drawing and plant nice flowers in this aquarium.

138. How many fish are here?

137. PROBLEM: This engine must change the place of cars A and B. Then, it must put them back in their places. But how? Clue: the engine can move forward and backward.

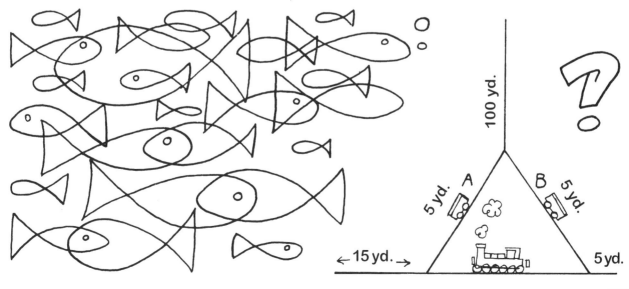

37

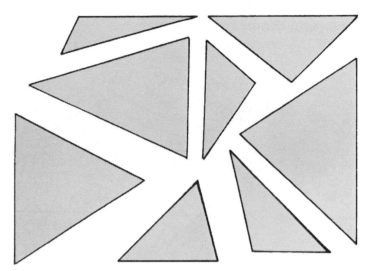

139. Which puzzle pieces don't belong to the drawing on the left?

140. Which are the misspelled words?

umbrel	pajama	joging	hyena	hyeroglyph	dolphin
shining	imediately		cathedral	april	masterpice

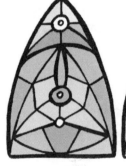

141. Two stained glass windows are identical. Which ones?

142. Find the way following the multiples of the numbers.

2	3	4	5	6
8	6	4	5	12
9	16	3	18	5
4	12	5	12	10
15	3	4	15	18
18	6	12	6	10
9	16	8	10	12

143. Join the numbers in the correct order and color the drawing.

144. How many leaves are there?

145. Circle the animals that hibernate.

146. Carefully copy the snowman on the grid to the right.

147. Write the months of each season.

Spring	Summer	Fall	Winter

148. The parachutist has jumped from the plane that doesn't resemble the others. Find the parachutist's plane.

149. Put your pencil on the arrow below the parachutist, close your eyes, and draw his way down to the landing point on the bottom of the page.

150. Across: 1. country in Europe whose capital is London 6. you can fasten your shoes with it 7. in the past; earlier 9. a measure of weight equal to 100 pounds (short hundredweight) 10. a detailed examination or investigation 11. a small round mark; a spot; a point 12. the sun god of the ancient Egyptians 14. at, in, or to this place 16. to go or put on board of a ship or an aircraft **Down:** 1. a correction made by rubbing out (pencil marks) 2. great honor and prestige 3. Los Angeles (abbr.) 4. one who accedes 5. state in north-east U.S.A. whose capital is Albany (2 words) 8. the first two letters of "guardian" 13. the first two letters of "America" 14. exclamation expressing surprise, happiness, triumph 15. the symbol of the chemical element Tellurium

151. Fill in the missing numbers.
The result of each row and column is 20.

152. Circle the misspelled words and correct them.

| hollyday | helth | newspaper | scisors | mistery |

spectecles   anouncement   bungallow   conztellations

immagination   pacefully   hypopotamy   costom

buket   chestnut   labortory

40

153. Find the way from 1 to 20 following the successive numbers.
Two successive numbers must be in two adjoining boxes.

1	2	3	4	7	8	9	10	11	10	11	14	15	17	18	19	18	17
2	2	4	5	6	8	10	11	12	13	12	13	15	16	17	18	19	18
3	3	4	5	6	7	8	9	10	11	12	13	14	15	16	17	18	17
4	5	6	7	7	10	9	10	11	12	15	16	17	18	19	18	20	
5	6	6	7	8	9	10	11	12	13	14	15	16	17	16	19		

154. Solve the problems.

$$3 \ldots 3 \ldots 3 \ldots 3 \ldots 3 = 72$$
$$3 \ldots 3 \ldots 3 \ldots 3 \ldots 3 = 21$$
$$3 \ldots 3 \ldots 3 \ldots 3 \ldots 3 = 78$$
$$3 \ldots 3 \ldots 3 \ldots 3 \ldots 3 = 51$$
$$3 \ldots 3 \ldots 3 \ldots 3 \ldots 3 = 26$$
$$3 \ldots 3 \ldots 3 \ldots 3 \ldots 3 = 36$$

155. The result of each row and column must be 30.

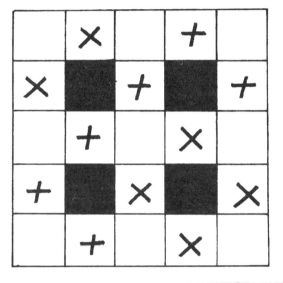

156. How can you go from 1 to 67 by passing through 22? Fill in the empty boxes logically.

1						22					67

157. Find the five differences.

158. What a mess! What instruments are here and how many?

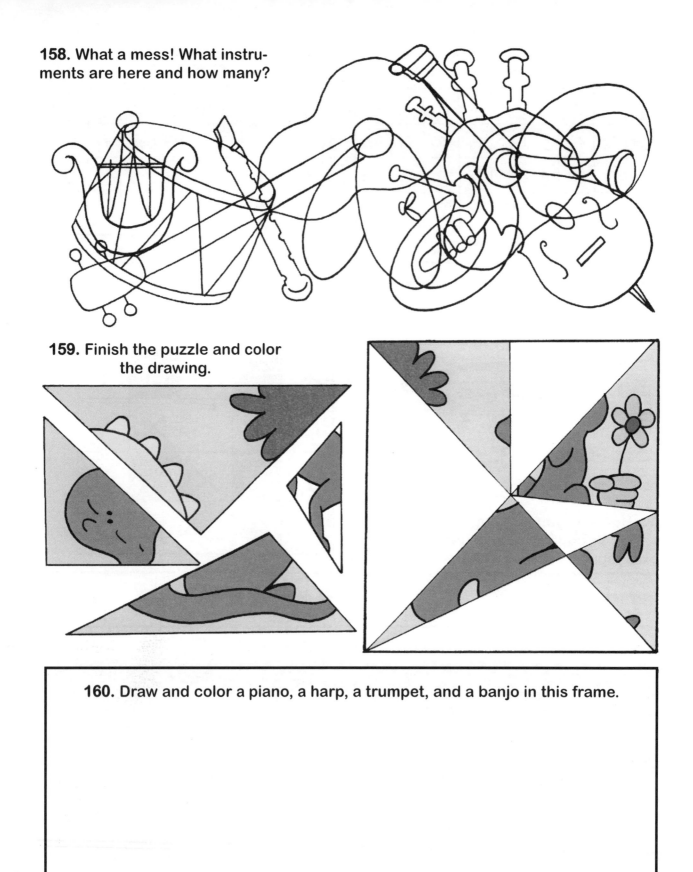

159. Finish the puzzle and color the drawing.

160. Draw and color a piano, a harp, a trumpet, and a banjo in this frame.

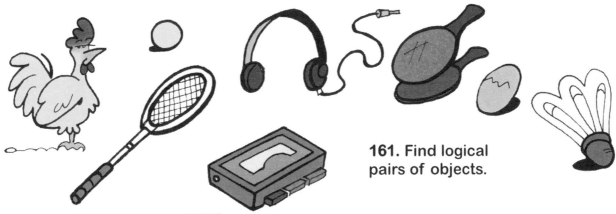

161. Find logical pairs of objects.

162. Find the five errors.

Which is the right detail?

163. Complete these math problems so that the results will be right.

1.
6... 6 ... 6 ... 6 = 5
6... 6 ... 6 ...6 = 8

2. 6... 6 ... 6... 6 = 13
6...6 ... 6... 6 = 42

3. 6... 6 ...6 ... 6 = 48
6...6...6 ... 6 = 66

4. 6... 6 ... 6 ... 6 = 108
6... 6 ... 6 ... 6 = 180

164. Draw a nasty ghost.

165. Find the shapes below in the opposite drawing.

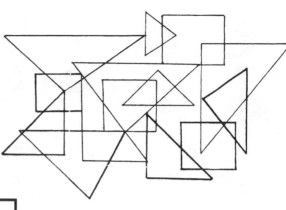

166. Number all the letters of the alphabet and write your name using this code.

167. Find the result by adding the figures that make up these numbers as in the model.

$1188 = 1+1+8+8 = 18 = 1+8 = 9$

$9696 =$

$2376 =$

$5694 =$

168. Collect the keys because they will help you open the doors.

169. Draw the various sides of the shape below.

top view

front view

side view

44

170. Arrange these fragments to form a square.

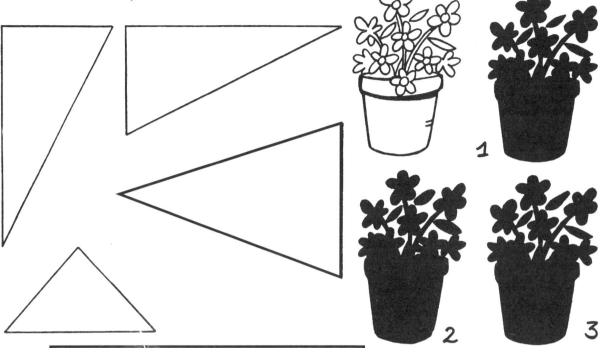

1

2   3

172. Questions for the champions.

1. In what years are the Olympic Games held?
2. Is there any athlete who has ever run 100 meters in less than 8 seconds?
3. Who is the fastest: man or the cheetah?
4. How many players form a volleyball team?
5. What's the name of the hockey "ball"?

173. Carefully copy the witch.

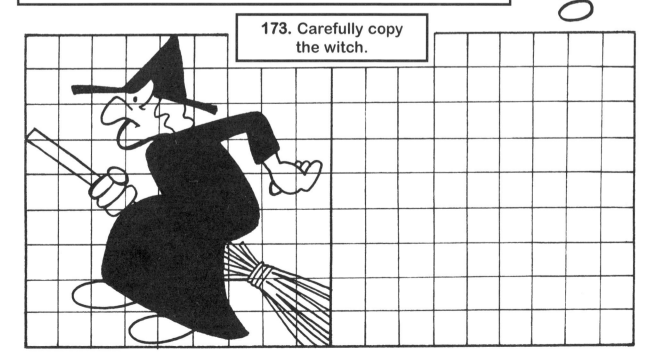

45

174. How many cups did the waiter drop?

175. Precisely draw the lady's order.

176. Do you know drinks starting with these letters?

P
C
L
M
S
W

177. The client gives the waiter a 100-dollar bill. How much is the change?

21 + 14 + 23 + 8 + 11 =

178. Find the fragments that will make a complete cup.

179. How many shells can you find? Color the ball below according to the math answers in 180.

180. Do the calculations and color the drawing following the results obtained.

3+1

7-5

4-3

9-6

181. Join the numbers in the right order and color the drawing.

47

182. Join the numbers in the right order and color the drawing.

183. What marine animals do these shadows represent?

184. Name fresh water and sea water animals.

185. Which tastes are represented below?

1 _____

2 _____

3 _____

186. What do we call these parts of the fish?

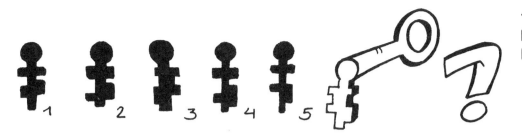

187. Which lock does this key fit?

188. From what stories do these characters come? Do you know them?

189. Which instrument doesn't belong here?

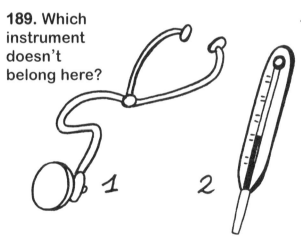

190. For what are these instruments used?

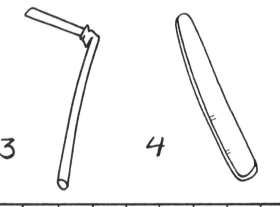

191. Try to make the pattern "OXO" every time you write an X or an O. How many times did you manage?

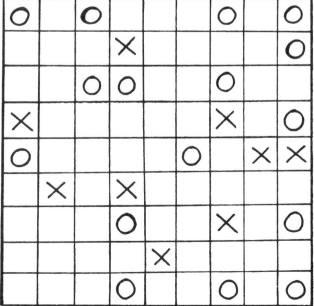

49

192. Whose shadow is this?

193. Check the right answer.

A. Who was Christopher Columbus?
○ An explorer
○ An inventor
○ A football player

B. What is New Zealand?
○ A town
○ A province
○ A country

C. Copenhagen is the capital of:
○ Sweden
○ Norway
○ Denmark

D. Where is Mexico found?
○ In North America
○ In South America
○ In Central America

E. The flag red-white-blue represents:
○ The Netherlands
○ Luxembourg
○ France

F. Luxembourg is:
○ A city
○ A province
○ A country

194. Find the shortest way out. You can break two walls.

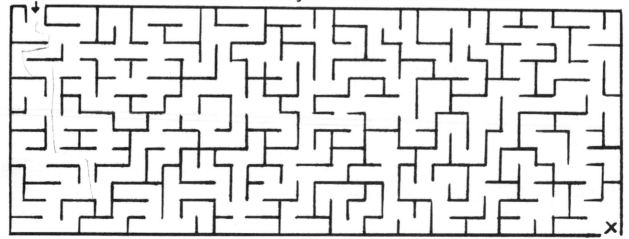

195. Join the numbers from 1 to 43 and color the drawing.

196. Calculate which target this live missile will hit.

$(30-1) \times 3 =$

62
91
87
74

197. The second clown wants to look like his friend. Help him put on make-up.

198. Find the twin lions.

199. The storm is near. How many clouds are there?

200. Draw Mr. Weather Forecast's map: "Several showers are to be feared in France. It's going to snow in England and it will be sunny in Spain. Stormy showers may come in the Scandinavian countries.

201. Solve the problems. What temperature is it?

+5
+4
×3
+3
÷5
−4
×2

°F

+7
−2
×4
−6
×2
÷4
+5

°F

+5
×6
−7
−3
÷5
+9
×2

°F

202. Transform this drawing into a rainy landscape.

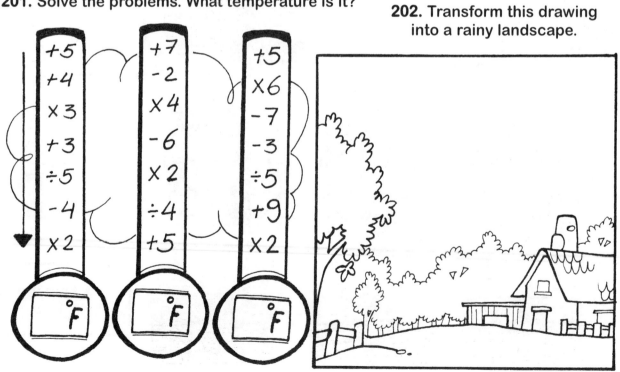

52

203. Find the plan of the pyramid.

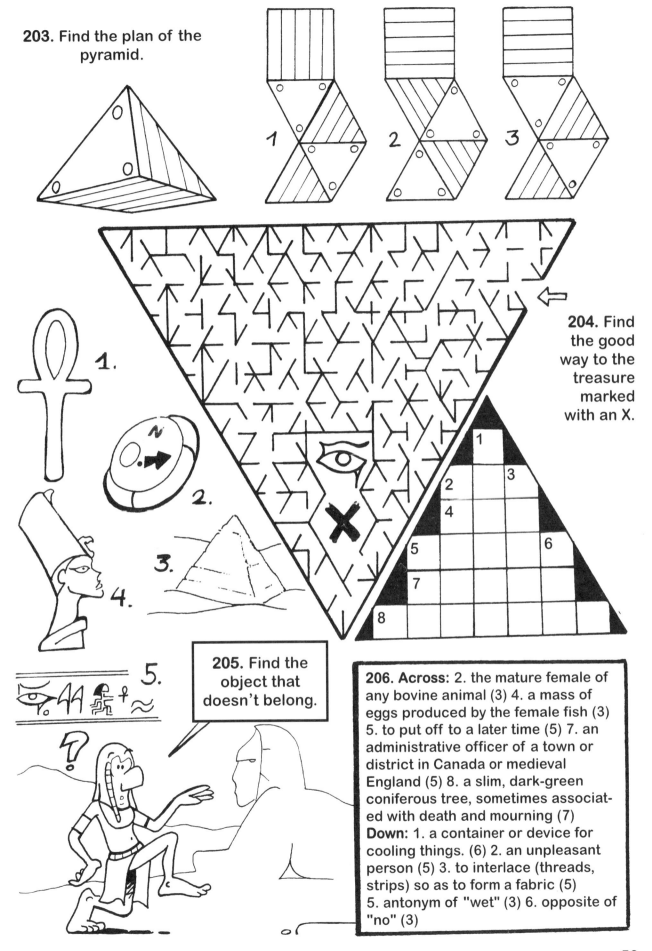

204. Find the good way to the treasure marked with an X.

1.
2.
3.
4.
5.

205. Find the object that doesn't belong.

206. Across: 2. the mature female of any bovine animal (3) 4. a mass of eggs produced by the female fish (3) 5. to put off to a later time (5) 7. an administrative officer of a town or district in Canada or medieval England (5) 8. a slim, dark-green coniferous tree, sometimes associated with death and mourning (7)
Down: 1. a container or device for cooling things. (6) 2. an unpleasant person (5) 3. to interlace (threads, strips) so as to form a fabric (5) 5. antonym of "wet" (3) 6. opposite of "no" (3)

207. Write letters in the empty boxes to make up words.

208. Join the numbers in the right order and color the drawing.

209. Write car brands starting with the letters...

P _____
M _____
J _____
F _____

210. Color this drawing.

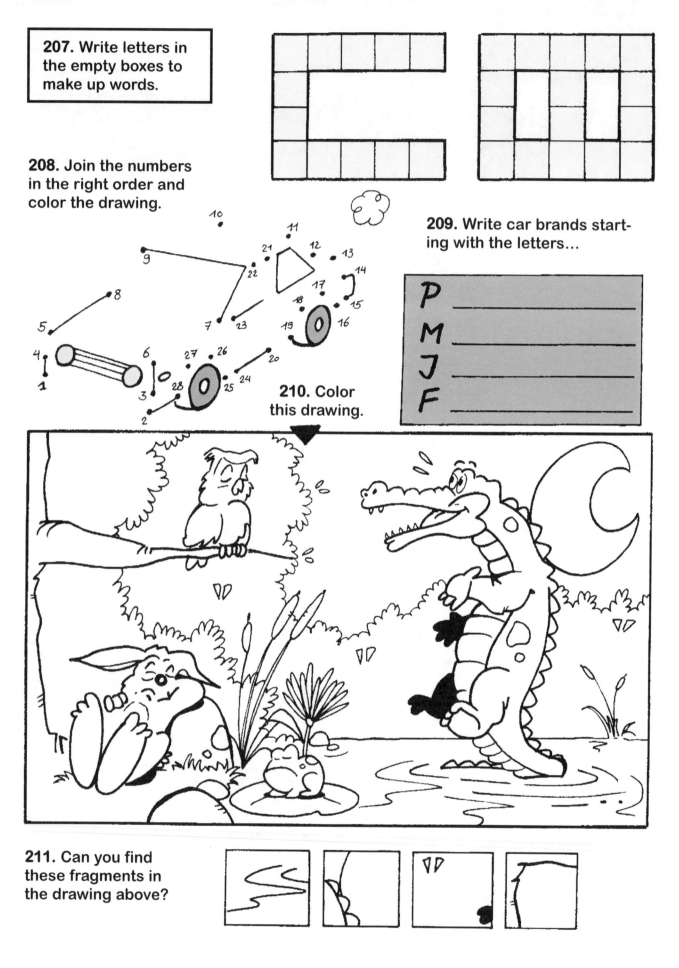

211. Can you find these fragments in the drawing above?

212. Which is the print of this seal?

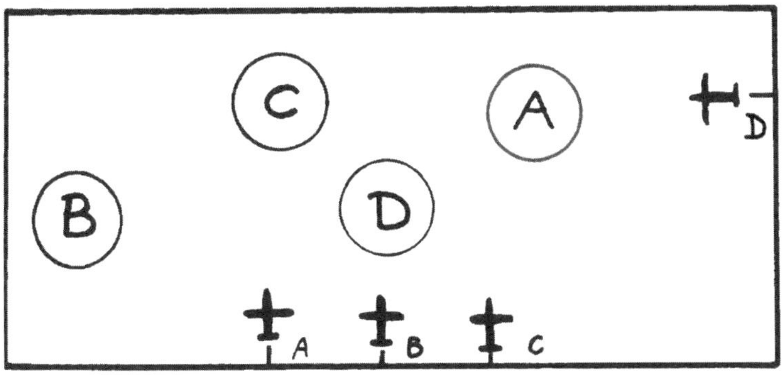

213. Each plane must land on its own runway. Draw the trajectory followed by each plane. Attention: their trajectories must not pass each other!

214. Form three triangles by removing three matches.

215. Form seven squares by moving three matches.

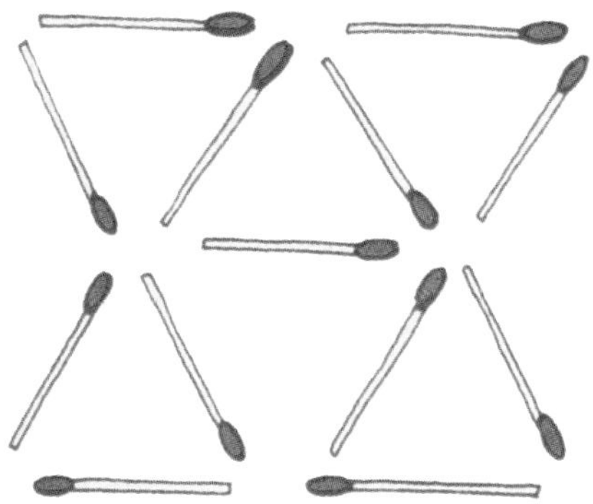

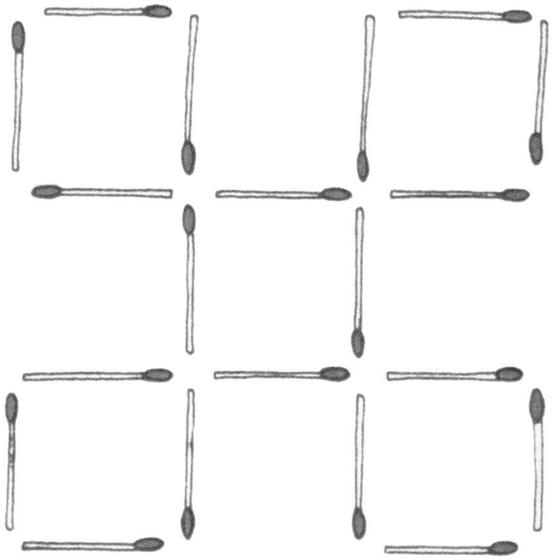

216. Help this worker find the right beam.

1

2

3

4

217. Precisely copy this cow head.

219. Solve the problems and circle the numbers representing the correct result.

$$174 - 42 = 131327$$
$$180 + 54 = 123456$$
$$64 \times 3 = 271928$$
$$384 \div 2 = 712192$$
$$288 - 97 = 181917$$

220. Which is the print of the seal?

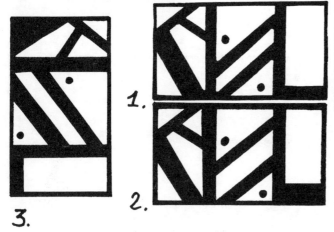

1.

2.

3.

221. Find the following words in the opposite diagram.

FIGURE COMPUTER COUNT
RESULT EQUAL PLUS
MINUS TOTAL SUM

218. Try to make the pattern "OXO" every time you write an X or an O.

O		O		X		O
			X		X	
		O			O	
				X	X	
O			X	O		O
				X		
O		O			O		O
	X	O	O				O
				X	X	
	X			O		O	O
	O			X		
X	O		O		O	
	X					X
O		X	O			O

C	O	M	P	U	T	E	R
O	F	I	L	Y	O	C	E
M	I	N	U	S	T	N	S
P	G	U	S	U	A	Q	U
U	U	S	A	M	L	W	L
T	R	W	C	O	U	N	T
E	E	Q	U	A	L	Z	E

56

222. Which of these funny birds cannot fly and therefore is an intruder?

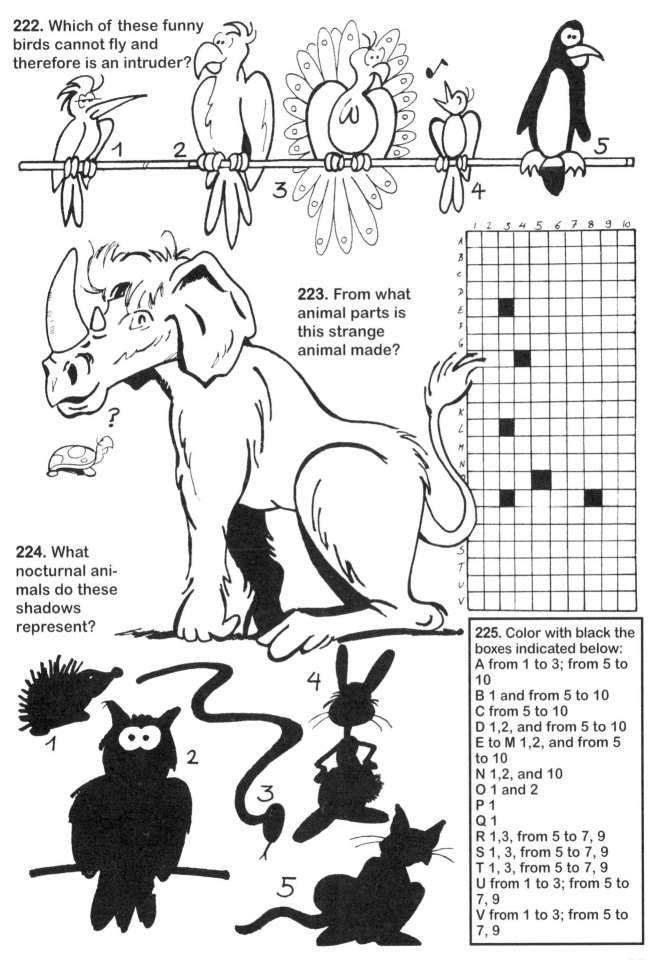

223. From what animal parts is this strange animal made?

224. What nocturnal animals do these shadows represent?

225. Color with black the boxes indicated below:
A from 1 to 3; from 5 to 10
B 1 and from 5 to 10
C from 5 to 10
D 1,2, and from 5 to 10
E to M 1,2, and from 5 to 10
N 1,2, and 10
O 1 and 2
P 1
Q 1
R 1,3, from 5 to 7, 9
S 1, 3, from 5 to 7, 9
T 1, 3, from 5 to 7, 9
U from 1 to 3; from 5 to 7, 9
V from 1 to 3; from 5 to 7, 9

226. Build your own robot.

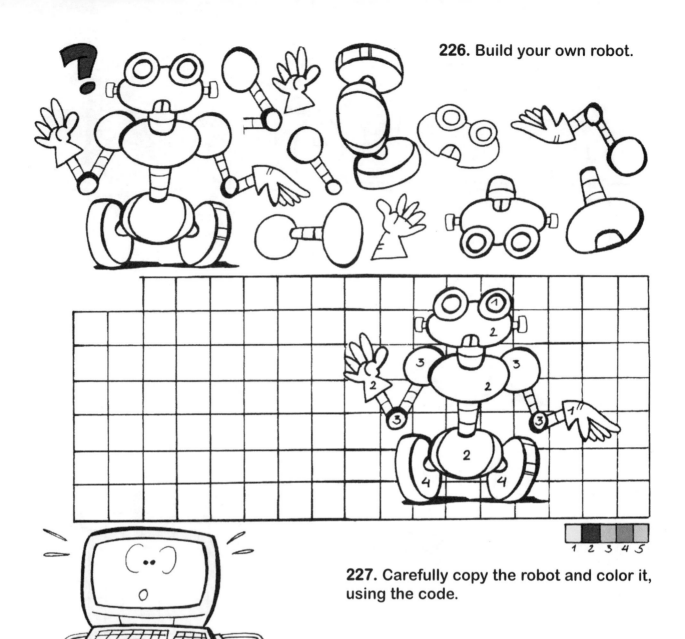

227. Carefully copy the robot and color it, using the code.

1 2 3 4 5

229. Try to make the pattern "OXO" every time you write an X or an O.

228. Solve the problems and take care to obtain the correct result.

$2 ... (4 ... 1) = 10$
$(8 ... 2) ... 3 = 13$
$5 ... (9 ... 3) = 8$
$10 ... (5 ... 1) = 2$
$(7 ... 4) ... 6 = 5$
$(9 ... 6) ... 4 = 12$

58

230. Give this lady and gentleman back their clothes.

231. Find the seven differences.

232. Draw a nice flowered dress.

233. Which shadow doesn't belong here?

1.

2.

3.

4.

5.

6.

7.

234. Which of the numbered lines extends to the left?

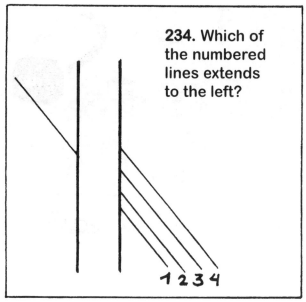

235. Which of the two triangles has the largest base?

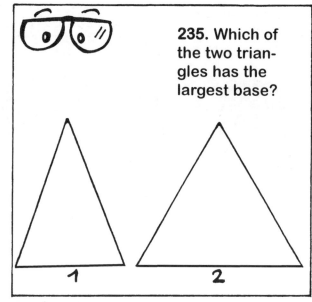

236. Imagine you are a bird flying in the sky. What do you see?

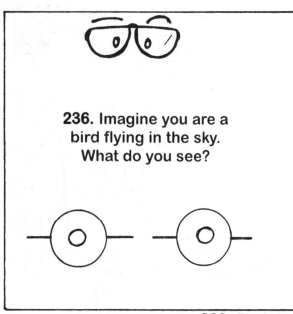

237. What does the bird flying above this scene see?

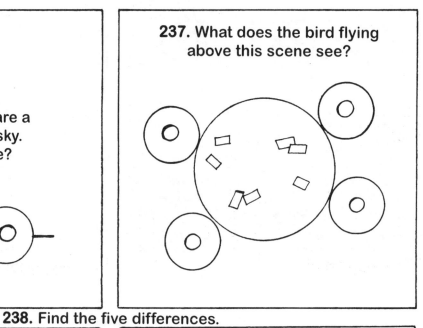

238. Find the five differences.

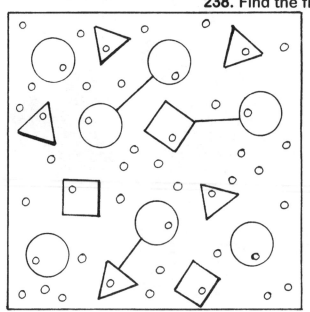

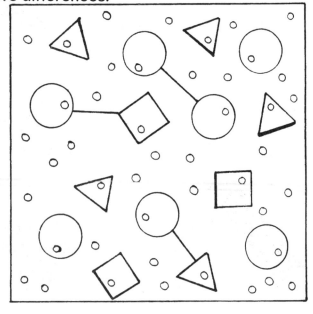

60

239. The soccer referee has two cards to penalize the players. What colors are they?

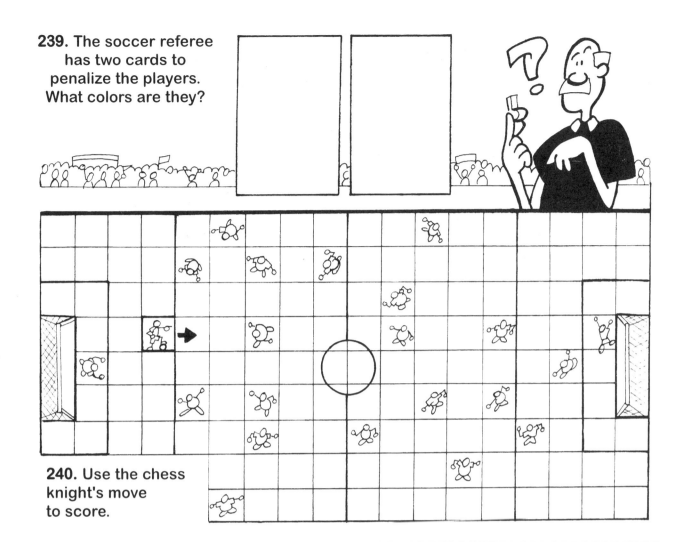

240. Use the chess knight's move to score.

241. A few tasks for basketball lovers.
Circle all the names of basketball players.

**Bryant   Sting   King   Clemens   Pippen
Bonds   Winfrey   Twain   Iverson   Spears
O'Neal   Timberlake   Miller   Roddick   Johnson
Knowles   Sosa   Gibson   Gordon   Griffey Jr.**

242. Join the numbers in the correct order and color the trophy.

ADVERTISING

243. Write below the car
brands starting with:

F _____

C _____

M _____

L _____

N _____

A _____

244. Create advertising for this
juice; you may also name it.

	cars	fruits & vegetables	animals	colors
R				
B				
O				
P				
F				

245. Fill in the boxes above with appropriate names:

246. Do you recognize the emblems of these car brands?

 1  2 3  4  5

247. Find the three differences.

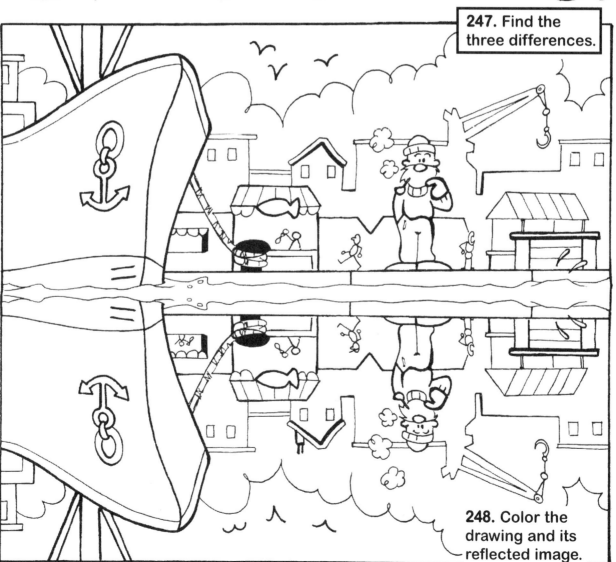

248. Color the drawing and its reflected image.

63

249. Across:
2. milk giver
5. baby cat
6. clawed sea spiders
9. female horse
10. animal kings

Down:
1. flightless bird
2. young horse
3. cobra, e.g.
4. last-century transportation
7. male cow
8. baby deer

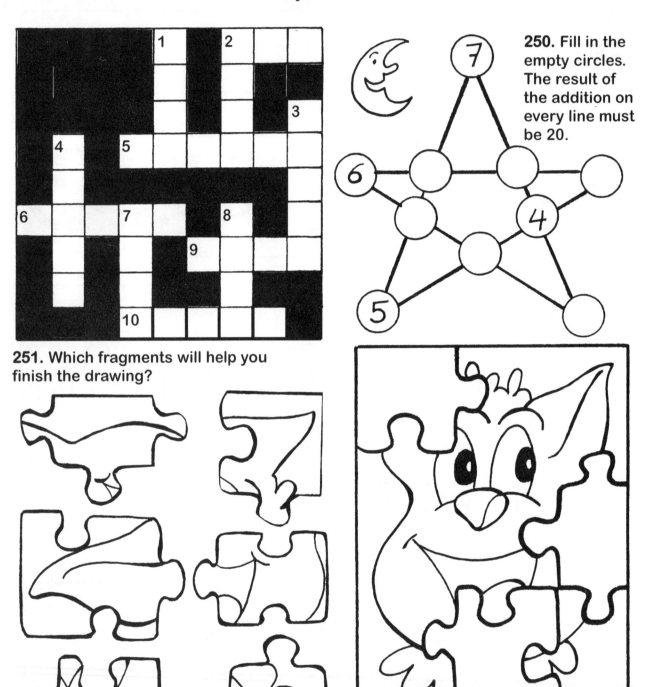

250. Fill in the empty circles. The result of the addition on every line must be 20.

251. Which fragments will help you finish the drawing?

252. Draw the pieces of the puzzle and color the picture.

253. Mark the right answers.

What's a koala?
○ a bear
○ a marmot
○ a cat

What's an elk?
○ a fish
○ a tiger
○ a stag

What's a zeppelin?
○ a car
○ a ship
○ an aircraft

What's a shepherd's purse?
○ a bag
○ a plant
○ a stag

What's a cello?
○ a musical instrument
○ a means of payment
○ a plant

What's a bassoon?
○ a string instrument
○ a wind instrument
○ a percussion instrument

What color is lavender?
○ purple
○ red
○ yellow

What does Pavarotti do?
○ paints
○ sings
○ governs a country

Where does Nelson Mandela live?
○ South Africa
○ South America
○ South Pole

Who was Kennedy?
○ a football player
○ a violinist
○ a president

Where is the Eiffel Tower found?
○ in Rome
○ in Madrid
○ in Paris

What does decathlon represent?
○ athletics
○ swimming
○ ball game

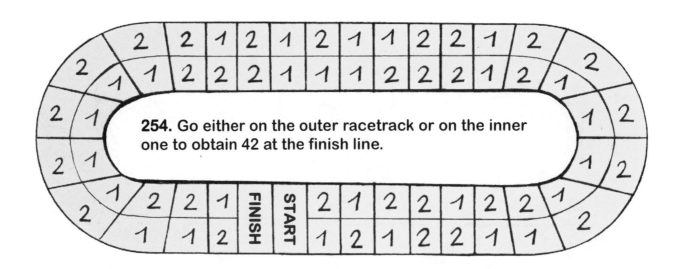

254. Go either on the outer racetrack or on the inner one to obtain 42 at the finish line.

255. Put your pencil on the athlete, close your eyes and try to jump the hurdles.

START.

256. Keep your pencil one inch away from the target, close your eyes, and try to hit it in the middle.

3
2
1

257. Put your pencil on the diver, close your eyes, and make him jump in the water by executing some dangerous flips.

258. What sport does each champion practice?

259. Do you recognize these three sports?

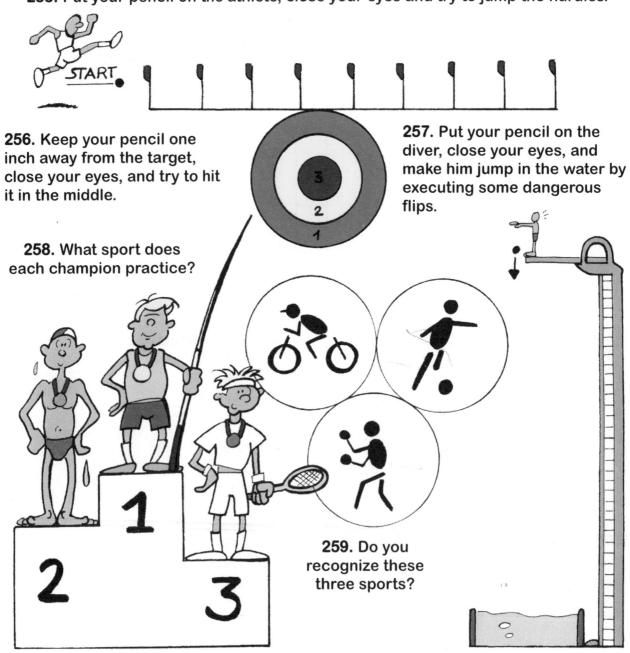

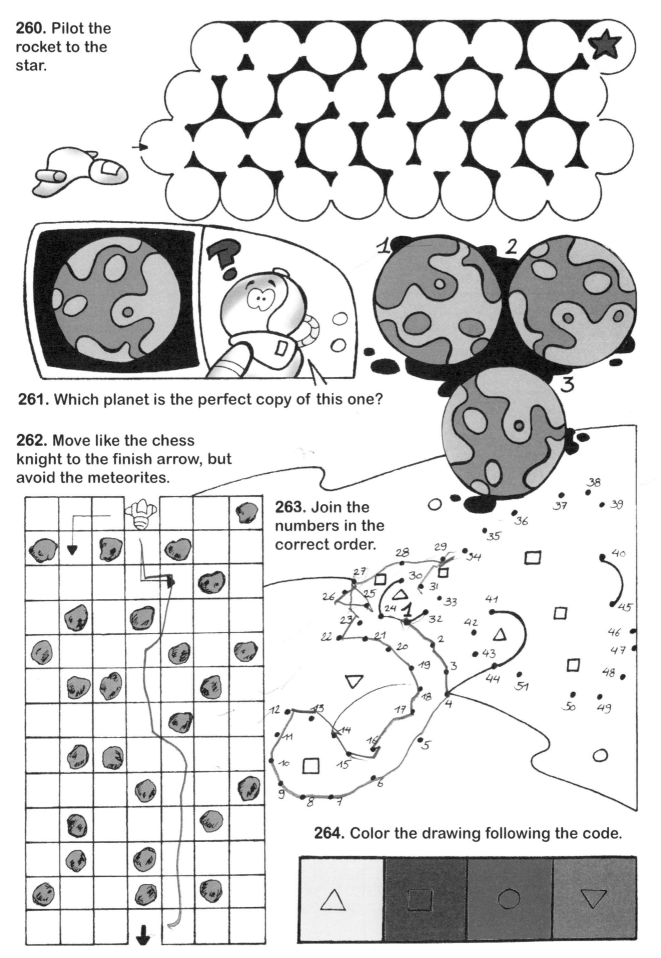

260. Pilot the rocket to the star.

261. Which planet is the perfect copy of this one?

262. Move like the chess knight to the finish arrow, but avoid the meteorites.

263. Join the numbers in the correct order.

264. Color the drawing following the code.

265. Draw the house of your dreams.

266. Write the various elements of a house below.

—

—

—

—

—

—

267. Give each character back his dwelling.

268. Where will you arrive if you follow the directions: straight forward - first street to the left - turn right at the lights - turn right at the second lights- at the end, turn left.

269. Draw the windows and the doors of this house and color it.

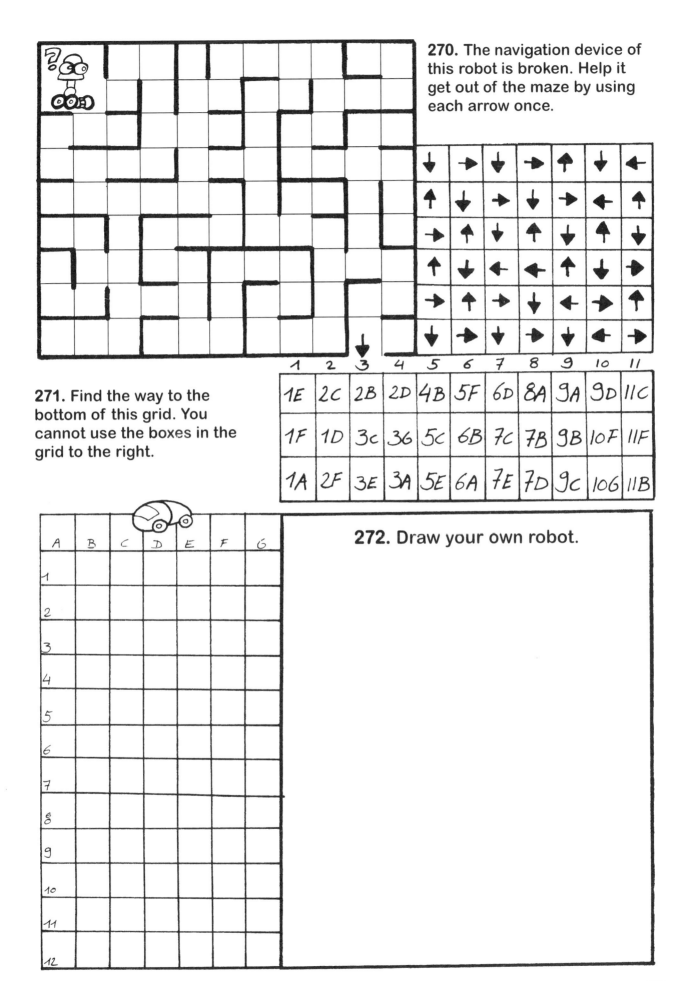

270. The navigation device of this robot is broken. Help it get out of the maze by using each arrow once.

271. Find the way to the bottom of this grid. You cannot use the boxes in the grid to the right.

1	2	3	4	5	6	7	8	9	10	11
1E	2C	2B	2D	4B	5F	6D	8A	9A	9D	11C
1F	1D	3C	36	5C	6B	7C	7B	9B	10F	11F
1A	2F	3E	3A	5E	6A	7E	7D	9C	106	11B

272. Draw your own robot.

	boys' names	girls' names	countries
A			
D			
M			
F			

273. Fill in this table, starting from the given letters.

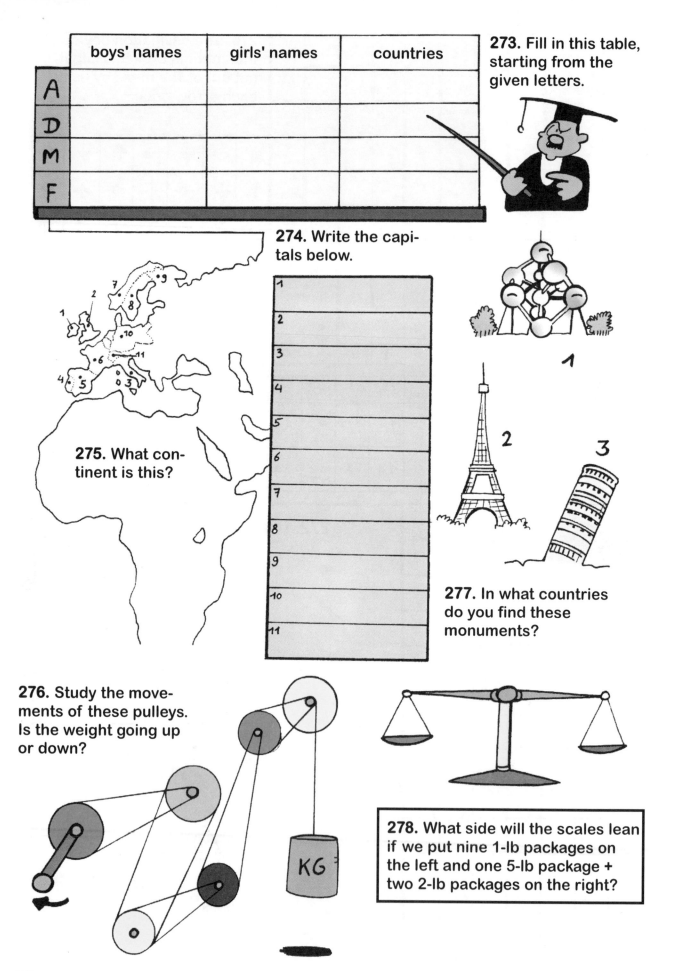

274. Write the capitals below.

1	
2	
3	
4	
5	
6	
7	
8	
9	
10	
11	

275. What continent is this?

277. In what countries do you find these monuments?

276. Study the movements of these pulleys. Is the weight going up or down?

278. What side will the scales lean if we put nine 1-lb packages on the left and one 5-lb package + two 2-lb packages on the right?

279. Problem: The farmer must carry the cabbage head, the lamb, and the wolf to the other side of the river, but he can carry just one at a time. He cannot leave the cabbage head and the lamb together because the lamb would eat the cabbage and the lamb wouldn't survive if left with the wolf. How can the farmer solve this problem?

280. Find the five differences and discover the artist's three mistakes.

281. Use the chess knight's move to guide the ship through the mines to the other bank.

Where do these three elements match in the picture above?

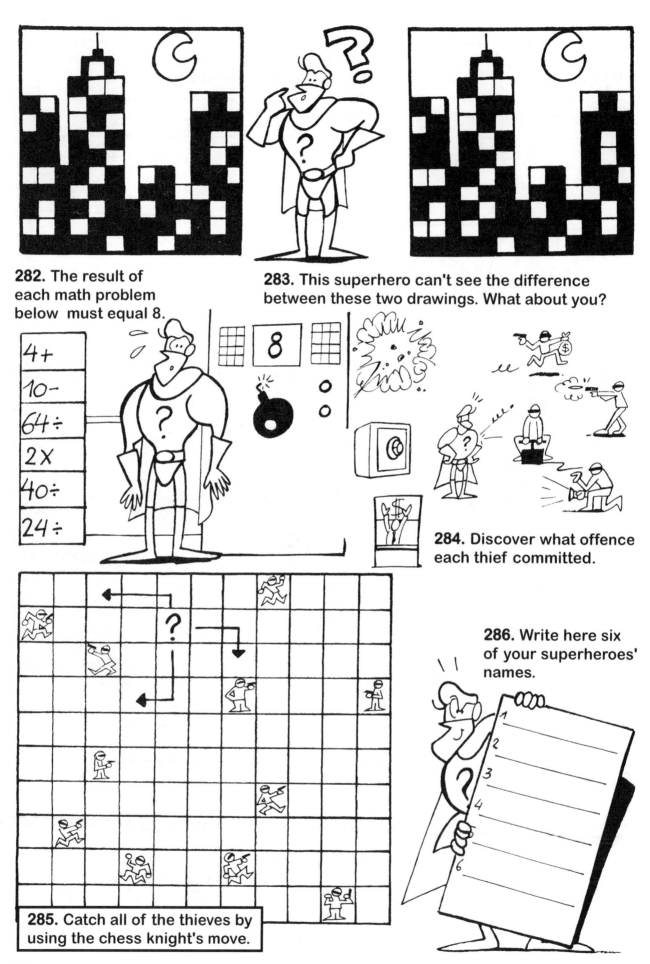

282. The result of each math problem below must equal 8.

4+
10−
64÷
2X
40÷
24÷

283. This superhero can't see the difference between these two drawings. What about you?

284. Discover what offence each thief committed.

286. Write here six of your superheroes' names.

1
2
3
4
5
6

285. Catch all of the thieves by using the chess knight's move.

72

	1	2	3		4	5	6	
7					8			9
10			11				12	
13		14			15	16		
17	18		19		20		21	22
23			24				25	
26		27			28	29		
	30				31			

287. Across: 1. angry; furious 4. prefix meaning "bad" 7. single, by one's self 8. antonym of "good" 10. innings pitched (abbr.) 11. _____ struck; completely amazed 12. knockout (abbr.) 13. sign of sadness; comes from the eyes 15. to know, in the past 17. brave 20. _____; cool and collected 23. opposite of "down" 24. estimated time of arrival (abbr.) 25. oath of allegiance (abbr.) 26. opposite of "nice" 28. bright; cheery 30. opposite of "yea" 31. estimated, for short **Down:** 1. to behave in a depressed, sulky or aimless way 2. same as "a" 3. used in addressing someone at the start of a letter 4. having a mild and gentle temperament 5. audio - visual (abbr.) 6. similar; to be fond of someone or something 7. started a fire 9. depressed; unhappy; dispirited; moody 14. everything 16. National Education Association (abbr.) 17. hobo 18. ready and willing to talk honestly; candid 19. to refuse to give or allow someone 20. to concern oneself about 21. wandering; not knowing where one is 22. month after April 27. Alcoholics Anonymous (abbr.) 29. operating system (abbr.)

288. Copy the Sphinx and color it.

289. Try to create the pattern "OXO" every time you write an O and an X.

73

290. Use these symbols in the indicated order to fill in these boxes. Which symbol will replace the question mark?

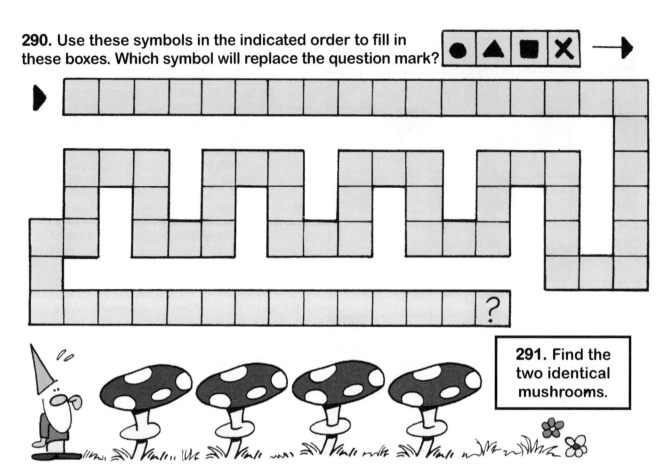

291. Find the two identical mushrooms.

292. Help the frog cross the pond. Put your pencil on the frog, close your eyes, and jump from one water lily to another.

293. Draw your pet. Color it.

294. Which of these animals give milk?

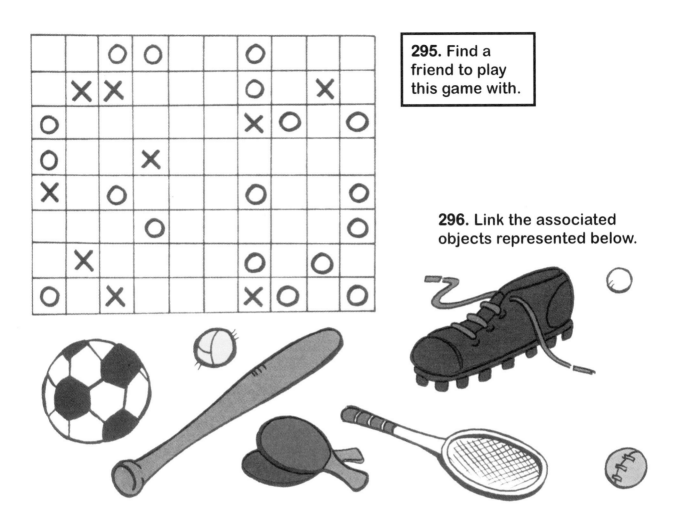

295. Find a friend to play this game with.

296. Link the associated objects represented below.

297. Find the mistakes in these sentences.

I drink a glass of milk now.

He doesn't know I'll be forteen tomorrow.

I wish my mother were here.

Will you be twelve tomorrow?

The teacher telles us to be quiet.

298. Find the three differences.

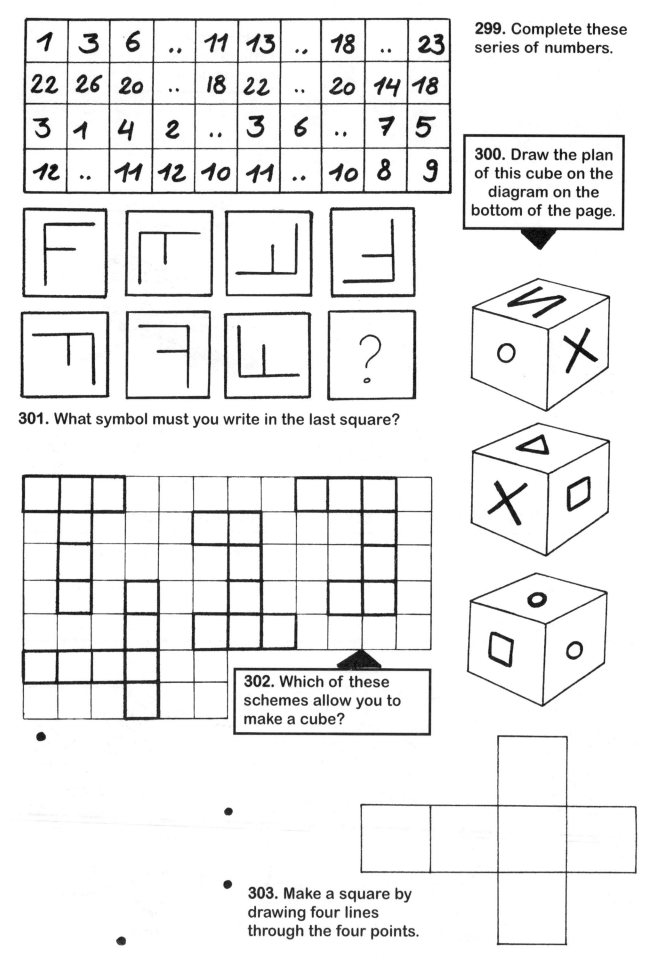

1	3	6	..	11	13	..	18	..	23
22	26	20	..	18	22	..	20	14	18
3	1	4	2	..	3	6	..	7	5
12	..	11	12	10	11	..	10	8	9

299. Complete these series of numbers.

300. Draw the plan of this cube on the diagram on the bottom of the page.

301. What symbol must you write in the last square?

302. Which of these schemes allow you to make a cube?

303. Make a square by drawing four lines through the four points.

76

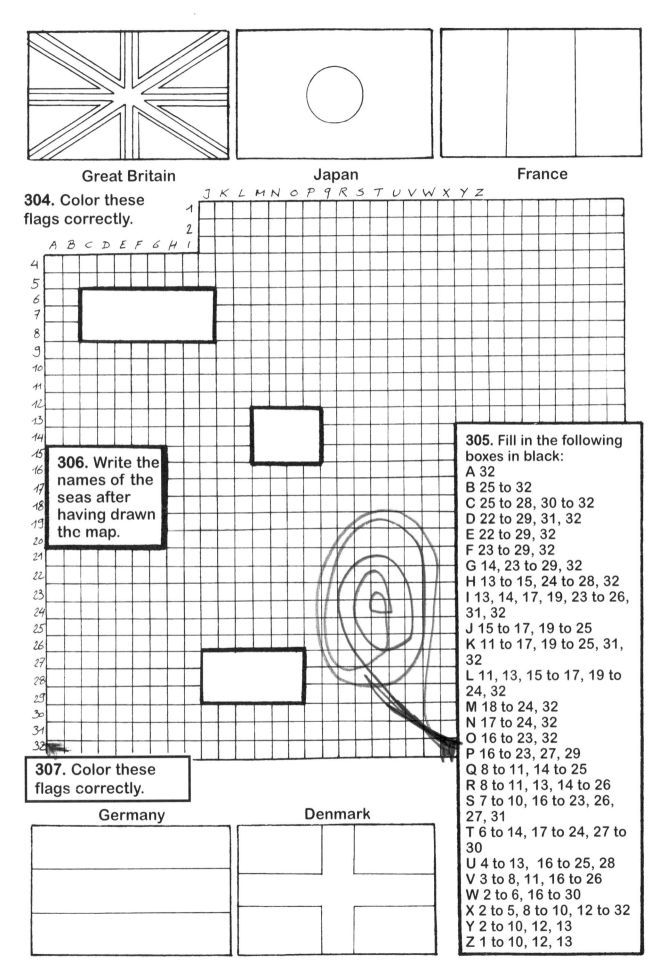

Great Britain

Japan

France

304. Color these flags correctly.

306. Write the names of the seas after having drawn the map.

305. Fill in the following boxes in black:
A 32
B 25 to 32
C 25 to 28, 30 to 32
D 22 to 29, 31, 32
E 22 to 29, 32
F 23 to 29, 32
G 14, 23 to 29, 32
H 13 to 15, 24 to 28, 32
I 13, 14, 17, 19, 23 to 26, 31, 32
J 15 to 17, 19 to 25
K 11 to 17, 19 to 25, 31, 32
L 11, 13, 15 to 17, 19 to 24, 32
M 18 to 24, 32
N 17 to 24, 32
O 16 to 23, 32
P 16 to 23, 27, 29
Q 8 to 11, 14 to 25
R 8 to 11, 13, 14 to 26
S 7 to 10, 16 to 23, 26, 27, 31
T 6 to 14, 17 to 24, 27 to 30
U 4 to 13, 16 to 25, 28
V 3 to 8, 11, 16 to 26
W 2 to 6, 16 to 30
X 2 to 5, 8 to 10, 12 to 32
Y 2 to 10, 12, 13
Z 1 to 10, 12, 13

307. Color these flags correctly.

Germany

Denmark

308. What countries or continents are these?

1

2

3

4

309. Who are these characters and from what countries do they come?

1   2   3   4   5

310. Indicate with numbers the order of the planets starting from the sun.

311. Write below the names of the planets of our galaxy.

1 _____

2 _____

3 _____

4 _____

5 _____

6 _____

7 _____

8 _____

9 _____

312. Indicate by numbers the order in which these planes and spacecraft were invented.

313. Guide Little Red Riding Hood through the woods. Beware of the dangerous wolf!

314. Here are the objects that Little Red Riding Hood took with her. Do you recognize them?

315. Find the two errors.

316. Illustrate the following story: Once upon a time, there was a castle enchanted by a witch. The castle was invaded by roses, and all of its inhabitants together with the beautiful princess fell deeply asleep. One day, a prince arrived at the castle on the back of his fine horse.

317. Which way do you have to go to get out of the rose garden?

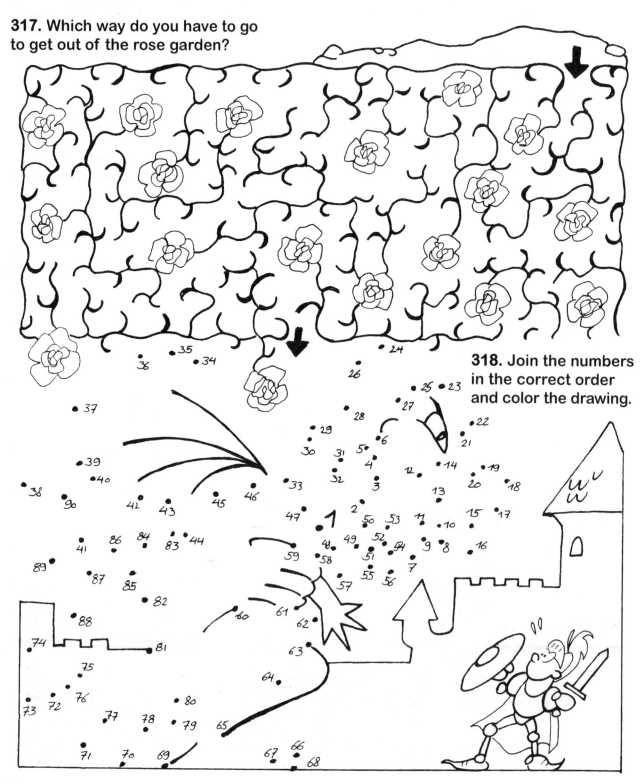

318. Join the numbers in the correct order and color the drawing.

319. Are there more or fewer frogs than flowers?

320. Find the error and color the drawing.

321. Can you find these details in the opposite drawing?

322. Which detail doesn't belong to this drawing?

323. Fill in the boxes with these symbols in the indicated order. Which symbol will replace the question mark?

324. Give each bird back the right egg.

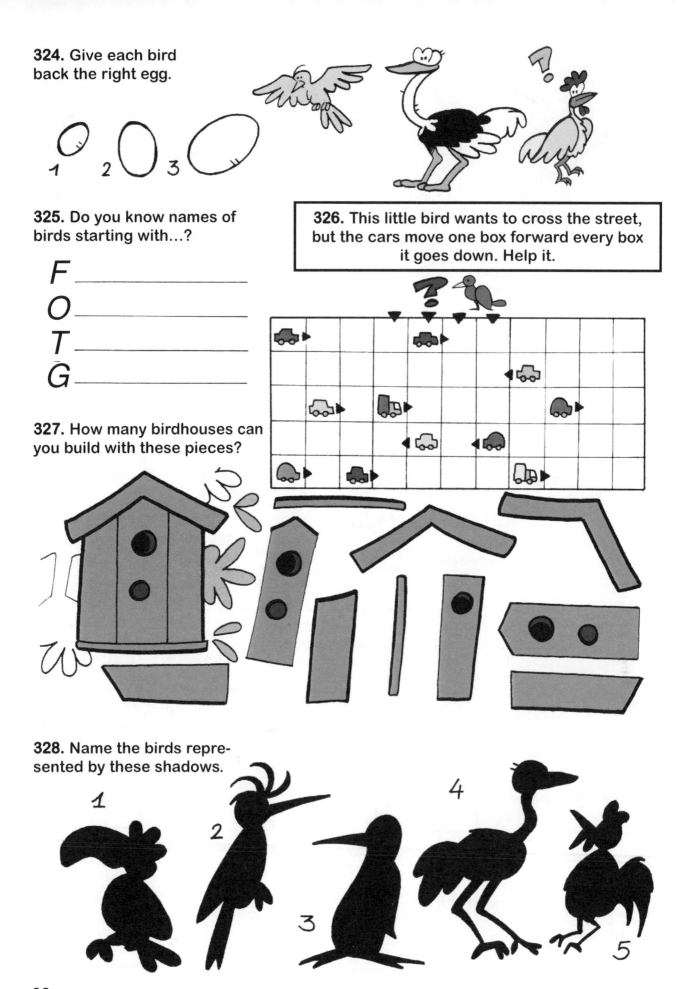

325. Do you know names of birds starting with…?

F _____
O _____
T _____
G _____

326. This little bird wants to cross the street, but the cars move one box forward every box it goes down. Help it.

327. How many birdhouses can you build with these pieces?

328. Name the birds represented by these shadows.

1

2

3

4

5

329. Remake a teddy bear with these pieces.

330. What colors will the last ball be, considering the colors of the previous balls?

red-yellow   yellow-blue

blue-red

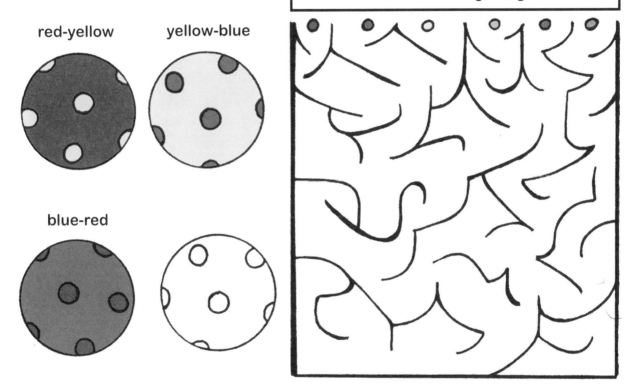

331. Which of these six balls can roll to the bottom without getting stuck?

332. Color these pictures to match the objects' colors in reality.

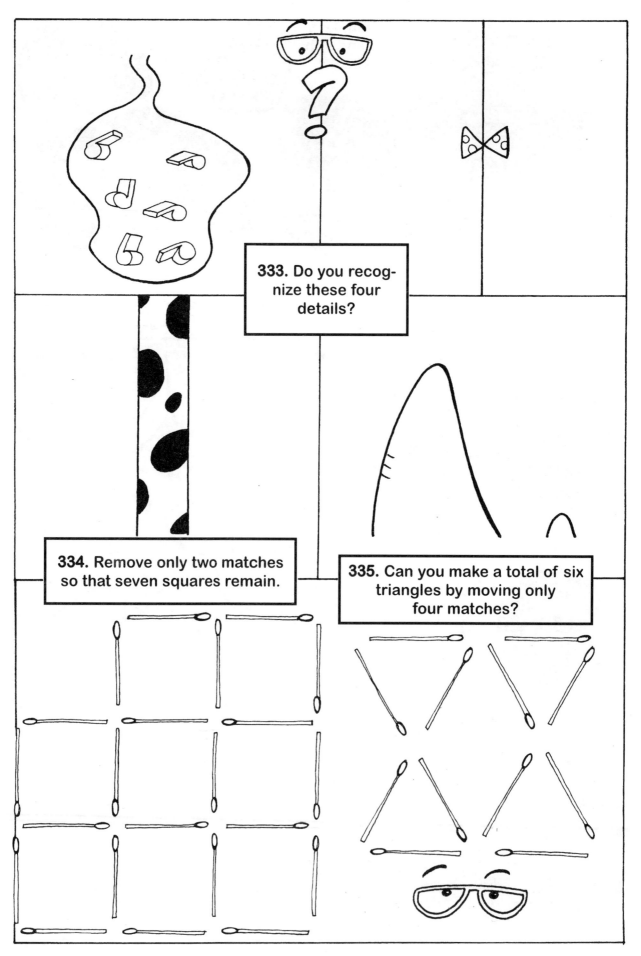

333. Do you recognize these four details?

334. Remove only two matches so that seven squares remain.

335. Can you make a total of six triangles by moving only four matches?

336. Questions for the champions.

1. Name five animals living in Africa.

2. Define the word "swamp."

3. What is the opposite of Northwest?

4. What do butterflies do with their antennas?

5. Why are some houses built on stilts?

6. What is a sphinx?

7. Is the dolphin a fish?

8. What is the warbler?

9. Who were the Wright brothers?

10. Name an endangered animal.

11. What animal is the mascot of the World Wide Fund for Nature?

12. What does Greenpeace protect?

13. What is an ecosystem?

14. Where do elephants live?

15. How many legs does a centipede have?

16. What is a top model?

337. Color this car.

338. Link the associated pairs of objects.

339. How many identical ducks can you find?

340. What a funny creature! From what animals is it made?

341. Imitate the sounds made by each animal on this page.

342. Fill in the empty boxes. The result of the rows and the columns must equal 16.

5	4	1	6

343. Who owns these hats?

1

2

3

4

5

344. Try to maintain the pattern "OXO" every time you write an O or an X.

345. Join all of these points with straight lines without drawing more than three lines.

346. What color will you obtain by mixing the following colors?

347. Which objects don't belong to this strange collection?

348. Join all of these points by drawing only four straight lines.

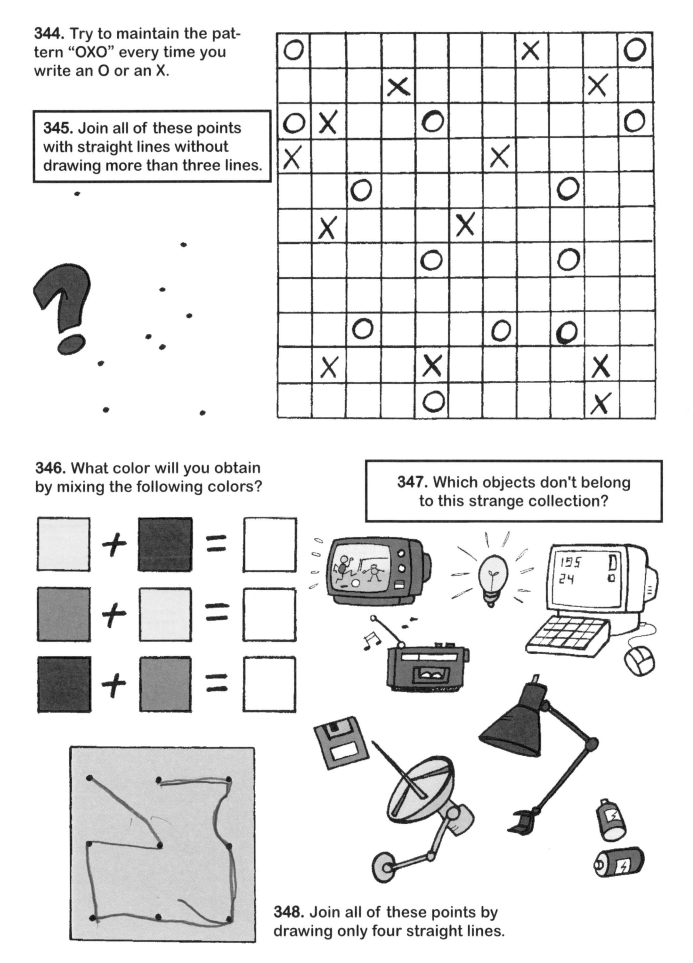

349. To whom do these sorts of helmets belong?

 1  2  3 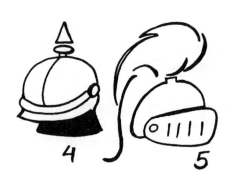 4 5

350. Draw a picture that the following words inspire in you:

cow
flower
car
tree
book
hedge
basket
child
man
chair
grass
goat
horse

351. Look carefully at the examples before completing these problems.

□ + ○ = △
△ − □ = ○
△ − ○ = ...
□ + □ = ...

□ − △ = 4
○ − △ = ...
△ + △ = 2
□ − ○ = 1

352. Two of these three cows
are twin sisters. Which ones?

353. Color the drawing.

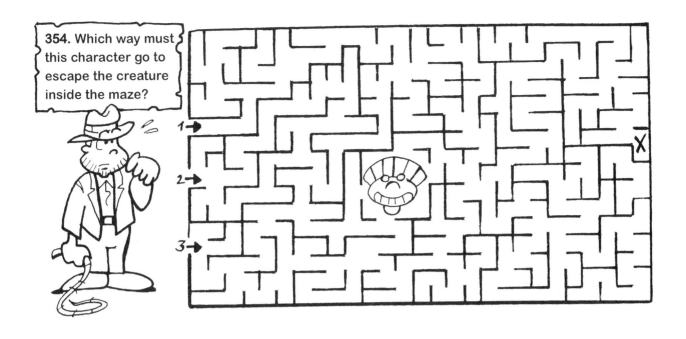

354. Which way must this character go to escape the creature inside the maze?

355. What animals have these shadows?

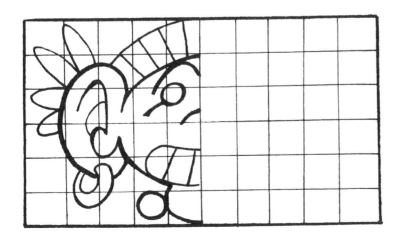

356. Draw the right side of this mask and color it.

357. Just one diamond can enter this case perfectly. Which one?

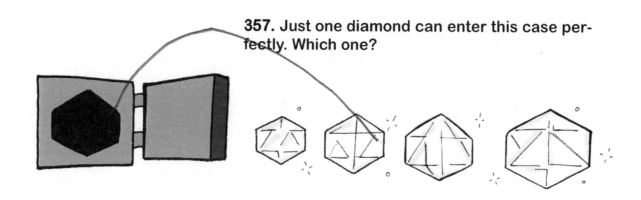

358. Find the elements that make the thief's portrait.

 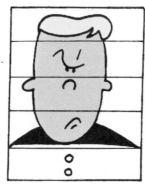  

359. Two digital fingerprints are identical. Which ones?

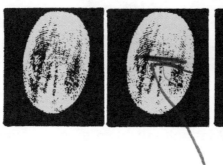 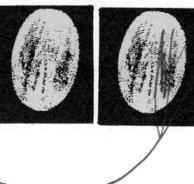

360. What creatures left these prints?

  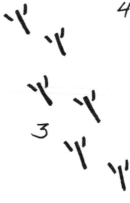 

1

2

3

4

5

361. Hurrah! Spring has come. The dwarf is very curious to see which flowers are going to grow. Help him by drawing the indicated flowers.

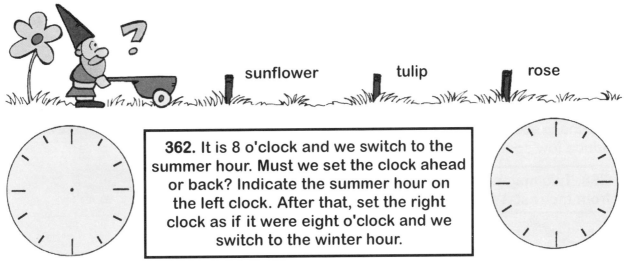

sunflower   tulip   rose

362. It is 8 o'clock and we switch to the summer hour. Must we set the clock ahead or back? Indicate the summer hour on the left clock. After that, set the right clock as if it were eight o'clock and we switch to the winter hour.

363. What are the names of these animals? Which live on the ground, which fly, and which live in the water?

364. Find the object that doesn't belong.

365. Find the drawing that the boy on the right is holding.

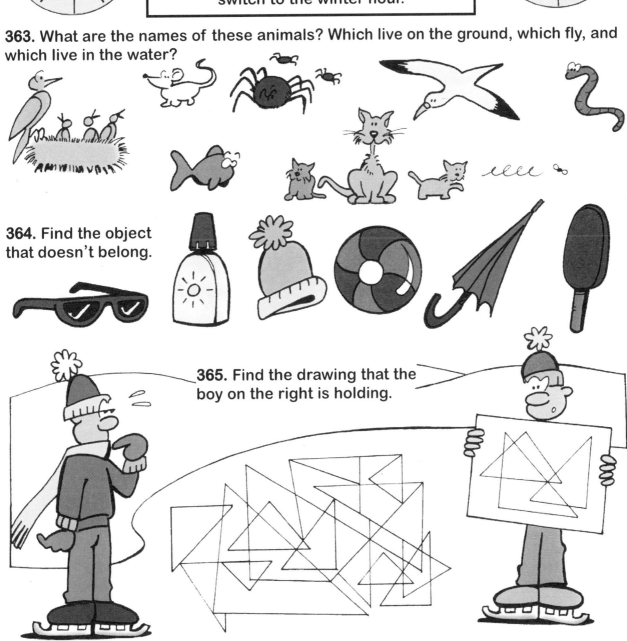

366. To which musical instruments do these shadows belong?

367. Which instruments produce sharp sounds? Which produce low sounds?

368. Two majorettes differ from the rest. Which ones?

369. Join the points from 1 to 26.

370. Color the drawing by using the codes below.

△ yellow   ○ blue   ▽ green   □ red

371. Fill in the empty boxes. The result of each row and column must equal 12.

372. Make the longest word using the following letters:

Y S L L
W O T N
O E E

373. Use the numbers given on the top line to fill in the empty spaces so that the results are correct.

2 7 10 25 5 4
= 64
= 20
= 11
= 86
= 231

374. Find the following animals:

pelican - ass
salmon - bear
anteater - magpie
turkey - goose
sheep - horse
boa - fox
cock - badger
fawn - lizard
pig - cat
hen - beaver
wolf - monkey
gnu - partridge

S	D	P	I	G	W	O	L	F	B	E	A	R
C	M	E	T	O	G	N	U	T	E	M	B	C
S	A	L	M	O	N	A	O	U	A	O	A	O
H	G	I	I	S	P	S	C	R	V	N	D	C
E	P	C	R	E	B	O	A	K	E	K	G	K
E	I	A	N	T	E	A	T	E	R	E	E	F
P	E	N	F	O	X	S	Q	Y	O	Y	R	A
L	I	Z	A	R	D	S	H	O	R	S	E	W
O	P	A	R	T	R	I	D	G	E	H	E	N

375. Finish the drawing using the puzzle pieces.

376. Color the drawing.

377. What ships belong to the same team?

378. Join the numbers from 1 to 30 in the correct order.

Color the drawing according to this code.

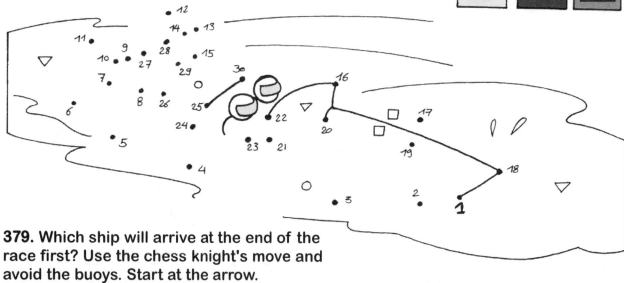

379. Which ship will arrive at the end of the race first? Use the chess knight's move and avoid the buoys. Start at the arrow.

380. Which craft does not belong to this series and why?

381. The window is broken. Can you find the fragments?

382. Which boot made this print?

1. 2. 3.

383. Whose shadow is this?

1   2   3   4

384. Help the detective get through the maze.

385. What's this detective's name after all? He has plenty of famous colleagues. Write their names on this list.

1 _____
2 _____
3 _____
4 _____

386. To what means of transportation do these shadows belong?

387. Which of these vehicles doesn't belong to the series and why?

388. Finish the drawing using the puzzle pieces and color it.

389. Color this drawing using your favorite crayons.

390. Can you find these elements in the drawing?

391. These two drawings differ in five elements. Which ones?

392. Find the missing fragment.

```
    15   18    13    14
         ▼     ▼     ▼
15 ↘ ┌─────┬─────┬─────┐
     │     │     │     │
17 ▶ │     │     │     │
     ├─────┼─────┼─────┤
     │     │     │     │
12 ▶ │     │     │     │
     ├─────┼─────┼─────┤
     │     │     │     │
16 ▶ │     │     │     │
     └─────┴─────┴─────┘
```

393. Use the numbers from 1 to 9 so that the calculations will be correct.

394. Mark the right answer for each question:

Who was Rubens?
○ a sculptor
○ a painter
○ a president

What is a chameleon?
○ an animal
○ a plant
○ a man

What is an igloo?
○ a captain
○ a fish
○ a dwelling

Who was Daniel Defoe?
○ a minister
○ a president
○ a writer

Where do penguins live?
○ at the South Pole
○ at the North Pole
○ at the South and the North Pole

Where do you find the pyramids?
○ in Marco
○ in Egypt
○ in South Africa

What is a reptile?
○ a snake
○ a rat
○ a fish

What is an orangutang?
○ a carnivor
○ a bird
○ a mammal

What is a scapegoat?
○ an animal
○ a man
○ a plant

What is an amphora?
○ a bird
○ a fish
○ a jar

What is jasmine?
○ a plant
○ a bird
○ a fish

What is an egoist?
○ a ship
○ an animal
○ a man

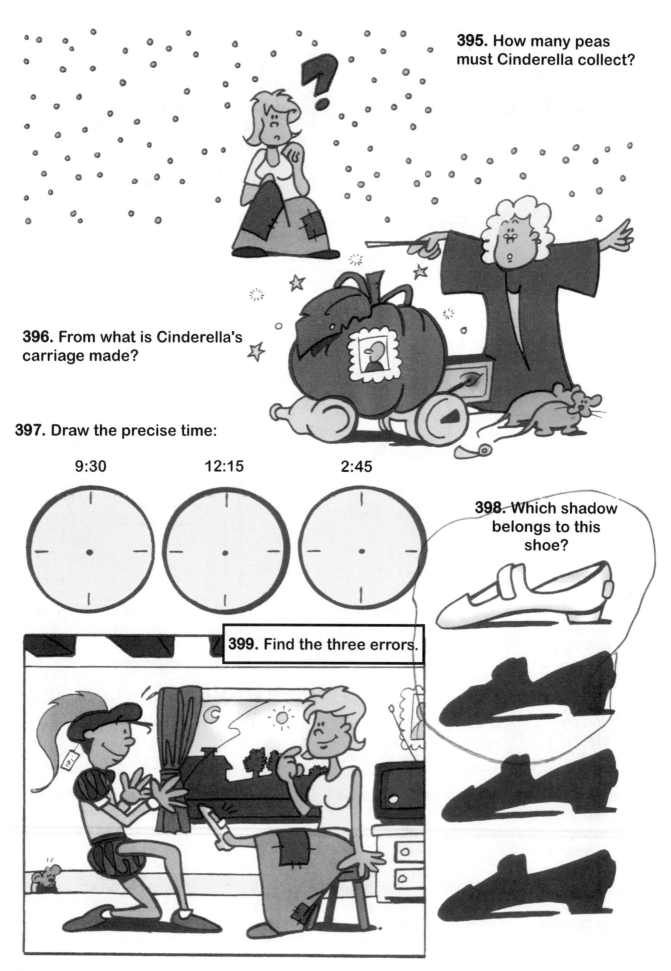

395. How many peas must Cinderella collect?

396. From what is Cinderella's carriage made?

397. Draw the precise time:

9:30   12:15   2:45

398. Which shadow belongs to this shoe?

399. Find the three errors.

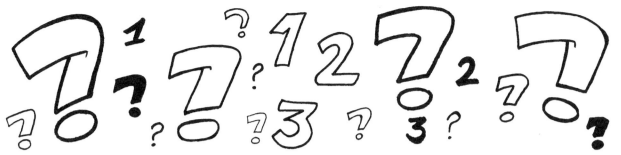

400. Mental calculation. You don't need to use your pocket calculator.

(500 - 200) x 2 =
○ 400
○ 500
○ 600

(5 x 6) + (6 x 5) =
○ 50
○ 60
○ 70

(8 x 8) - 10 =
○ 46
○ 54
○ 60

(900 - 450) x 2 =
○ 500
○ 900
○ 1000

850 - 100 - 50 - 100 =
○ 500
○ 600
○ 650

3 x 3 x 3 =
○ 25
○ 27
○ 29

(5 x 5) - (20 + 5) =
○ 0
○ 5
○ 10

(800 + 200) - 800 + 200 =
○ 400
○ 600
○ 800

950 - 250 + 300 =
0 900
0 950
0 1000

10 + 80 + 100 + 250 + 20 =
○ 450
○ 460
○ 480

(750 + 250) - (800 + 200) =
○ 0
○ 100
○ 1000

320 - 30 - 90 + 100 + 200 =
○ 480
○ 490
○ 500

845 - 55 - 45 - 45 - 25 =
○ 625
○ 635
○ 675

(325 x 2) + 325 =
○ 965
○ 975
○ 985

(3 x 2 x 5) - (5 x 3 x 2) =
○ 10
○ 20
○ 30

(68 - 23 - 15 - 7) x 2 =
○ 42
○ 44
○ 46

(36 - 2) x (28 - 8) =
○ 650
○ 680
○ 690

(1000 - 950) x (950 - 900) =
○ 2500
○ 500
○ 750

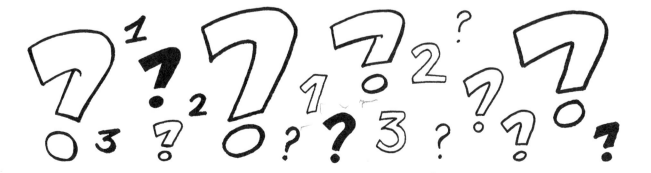

ANSWER KEY

1. vine #4

2.

3.

5. 28 - 6 = 22; 14 ÷ 7 = 2; 2 x 5 = 10; 5 - 3 = 2; 7 + 2 = 9; 3 x 4 = 12.

8. **9.**

10.

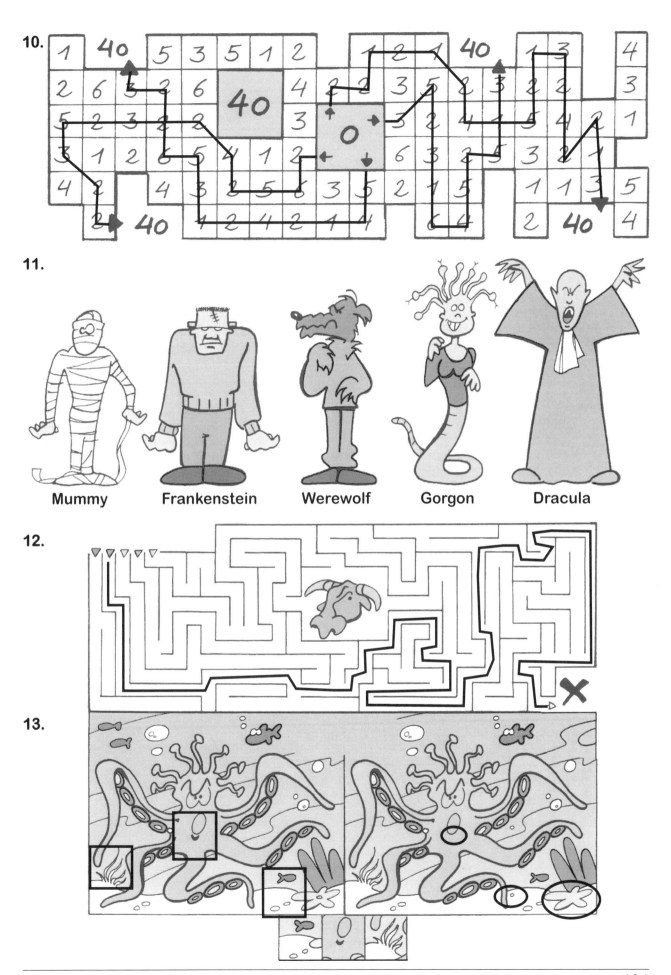

11.

Mummy Frankenstein Werewolf Gorgon Dracula

12.

13.

14.

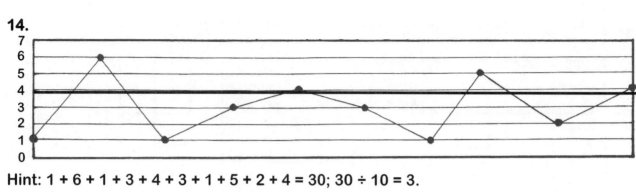

Hint: 1 + 6 + 1 + 3 + 4 + 3 + 1 + 5 + 2 + 4 = 30; 30 ÷ 10 = 3.

15.

apple tree   palm tree   pine

16. Fruits:
1. lemon
2. banana
3. apple
4. watermelon

18. Baloon # 2 is the closest; baloon # 3 is the most remote.

17.

	A	B	Y	S	S	A	L
A						O	E
D		O		U	N	I	T
V	I	K	I	N	G		T
A	D			I		F	U
N	E	O		C	H	I	C
C	A	F	F	E	I	N	E
E	L	F		F		E	

19.

1	2	5	6	7	8	9	10
2	3	4	5	6	7	8	11
5	4	5	6	7	8	9	12
6	7	10	11	12	9	10	13
7	8	9	13	14	10	11	12
8	13	14	13	16	17	18	13
9	12	15	14	15	20	19	14
10	11	16	17	16	17	16	15

20.

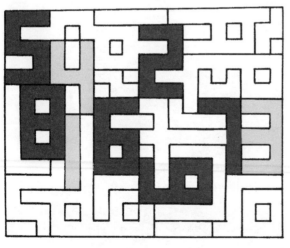

21.

23. 5x5+5-5=25; (5÷5+5)x5=30; 5-(5÷5)+5=9; 5x5+5x5=50; (5+5+5)x5=75; (5+5÷5)+5=11; 5+5+5-5=10; 5x5x5-5=120; (5+5)x5-5=45.

24.

25. The engines must follow the steps below:

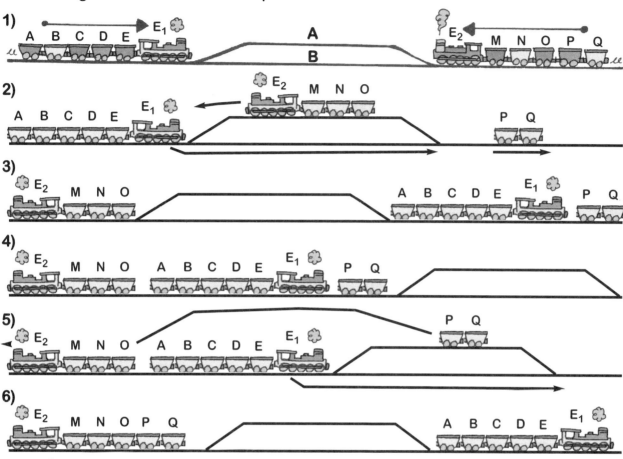

E₁ = engine #1   A, B, C, D, E = cars attached to E₁
E₂ = engine #2   M, N, O, P, Q = cars attached to E₂
Note that an engine can move cars backward and forward.

26.

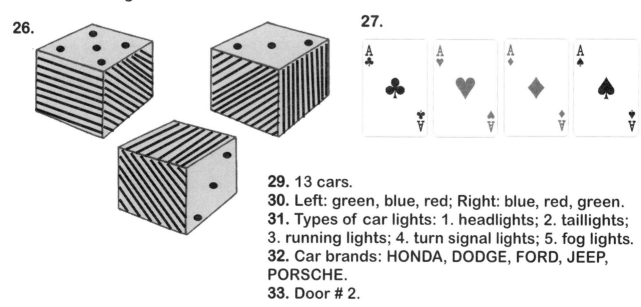

27.

29. 13 cars.
30. Left: green, blue, red; Right: blue, red, green.
31. Types of car lights: 1. headlights; 2. taillights;
3. running lights; 4. turn signal lights; 5. fog lights.
32. Car brands: HONDA, DODGE, FORD, JEEP,
PORSCHE.
33. Door # 2.

34.

 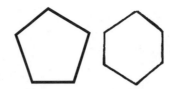

35. The frog must start from number 2.
36. ((9+6)-(4+5))+4=10;
((9÷3)+(2+3))-2=6;
(10-2-1)+(3x3)=16.

39.

40. Wheel # 2.
42. Object # 3.
43.

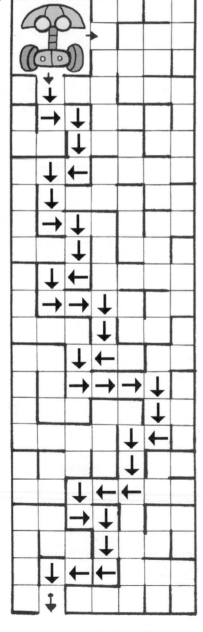

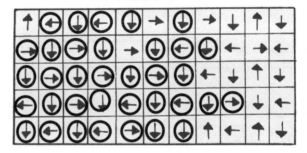

44. The identical fragment is in the corner lower left.

45.

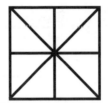

47-48.

46. Averages:
1) 10/10 + 2/5 + 4/10 + 3/15 = 1 + 2/5 + 2/5 + 1/5 = 1 + 5/5 = 2;
the average is:
    2 ÷ 4 = 1/2
2) 1/4 + 3/4 +1/2 +1 = 2 + 1/2 = 4/2 + 1/2 = 5/2;
the average is:
    (5/2) ÷ 4 = 5/8
3) 1/3 + 1/3 + 2/3 + 2/3 = 6/3 = 2;
the average is:
    2 ÷ 4 = 1/2
4) 1/4 + 1/4 + 1/4 +1 = 1 + 3/4 = 7/4;
the average is:
    (7/4) ÷ 4 = 7/16

49. 3 + 5 - 2 - 4 + 5 = = 7
50. Shadows: 1. bat 2. skull; 3. spider

51.

52. 14 bricks.

53.

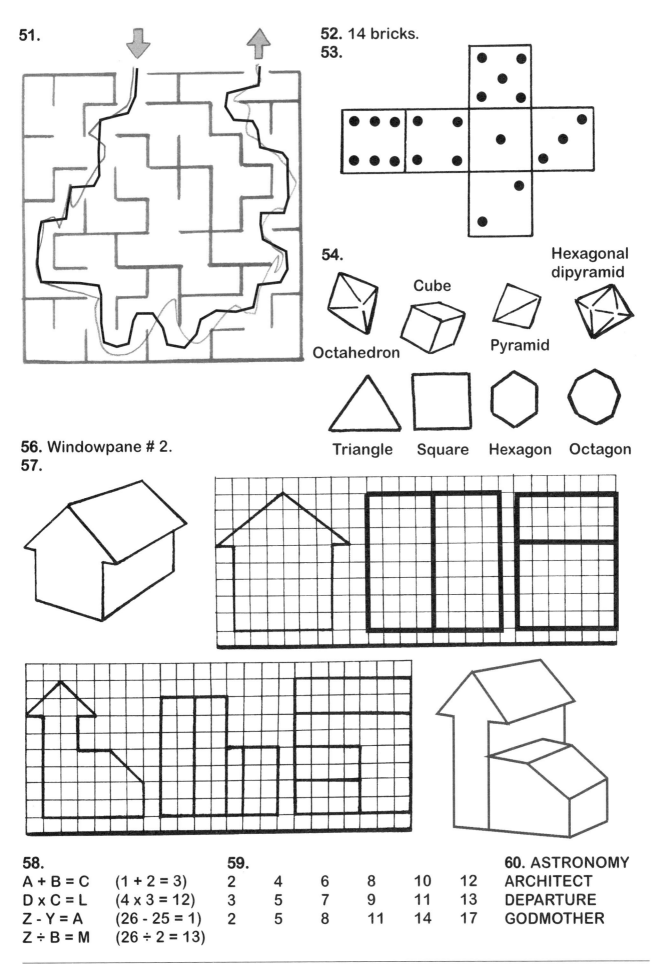

54.

Octahedron Cube Pyramid Hexagonal dipyramid

Triangle Square Hexagon Octagon

56. Windowpane # 2.

57.

58.

A + B = C	(1 + 2 = 3)
D x C = L	(4 x 3 = 12)
Z - Y = A	(26 - 25 = 1)
Z ÷ B = M	(26 ÷ 2 = 13)

59.

2	4	6	8	10	12
3	5	7	9	11	13
2	5	8	11	14	17

60. ASTRONOMY
ARCHITECT
DEPARTURE
GODMOTHER

61. Human face parts:
1. eyebrow 2. eye 3. nose 4. mouth 5. chin
1. forehead 2. ear 3. cheek 4. neck 5. throat

62.

63.

4	6	14		2	3	4
12	12	0		1	5	3
8	6	10		6	1	2

65.

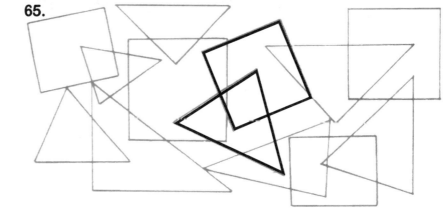

64. JOHANNESBURG
66. Shadows of
1. windmill 2. igloo
3. house 4. tepee (tipi).
Doesn't belong: wind-
mill - not a home

67.

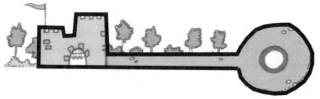

68.

70.

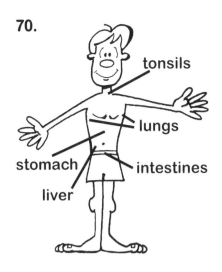

tonsils
lungs
stomach
intestines
liver

71. Are not blood types: D⁺, C⁺.

72.

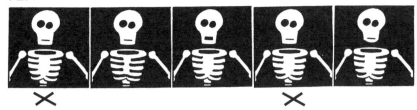

73. Instruments # 1 and # 3 don't belong in the surgical kit.

74. Ways to give medicine: 1. pills 2. syrup 3. injection

75.

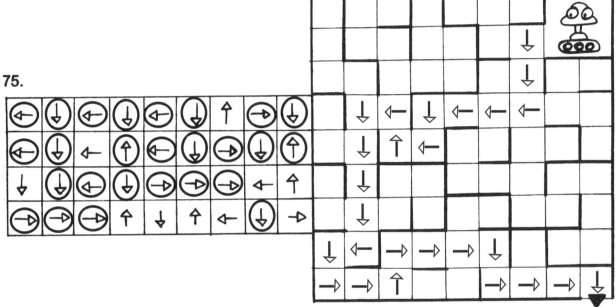

76.

→	1	2	3	①	2	2	4	1	⑤	2	2	5	④	1	5	3	**35**
→	4	3	1	3	4	2	②	3	2	4	①	4	3	2	3	4	**30**
→	2	2	②	4	⑤	3	3	1	1	1	3	1	5	①	5	2	**20**
→	③	1	2	5	2	1	3	2	4	4	3	2	2	3	4	①	**㉕**

→	1	2	3	1	2	2	4	1	5	2	②	5	4	1	5	3	**35**
→	④	3	1	3	4	2	2	3	②	4	1	4	3	②	3	4	**30**
→	2	2	②	4	5	3	③	1	1	1	3	①	5	1	5	②	**⑳**
→	3	1	2	5	②	1	3	2	4	4	3	2	2	3	4	1	**25**

77. Answer: 1, 2, 3, 5

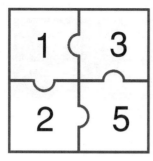

78.

79. Fisherman # 4.

80. To go fishing you need items 1, 2, 4, 5; you don't need item 3.

81.

3	+	4	+	3
+	■	+	■	+
2	+	5	+	3
+	■	+	■	+
5	+	1	+	4

82.

3	x	3	+	1
x	■	+	■	+
3	+	4	+	3
+	■	+	■	x
1	+	3	x	3

83. Foods come from
1. France 2. Italy
3. China 4. U.S.A.

84. 8 slices.

85. Dishes (suggestion): Pizza, Hamburger, Sushi, Lasagna

86.

89. BAKER; BALL; BALLET; BANANA; BLONDE; BOOK; BREEZE; CHATTERING; CORKSCREW; EMBERS; HYACINTH; HYENA; HYGIENE; INCOMPLETE; INNOCENT; KILO; KILT; KIMONO; LENGTH; LONG; LONGITUDE; MASHED POTATOES; MEANS; MEASURE; MERIT; MILLION; MONTHLY; ORNAMENT; PICTURE; PIGGY BANK; PIROGUE; PIROUETTE; RABBIT; SLOWLY; SQUIRREL; TARGET; TENT; UNCONSCIOUS; WAGON; WAPITI; WATER POLO; WATT; WAX CHERRY.

90. SINGERS
Madonna
Pink Floyd
Kylie Minogue
Jim Morrison
Elvis Presley

91. SONGS (suggestion)
Music
Another Brick In The Wall
I Should Be So Lucky
Hello, I Love You
Hound Dog

92.

93. Funny animal: deer horns, lion head, fish body, horse front legs.

95. Wheels and handlebars from 1. car 2. bicycle 3. motorcycle 4. airplane

96.

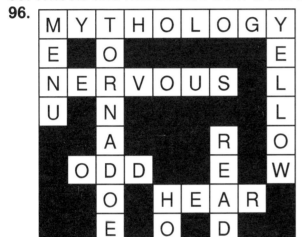

M	Y	T	H	O	L	O	G	Y
E		O						E
N	E	R	V	O	U	S		L
U		N						L
		A				R		O
O	D	D				E		W
O		O		H	E	A	R	
E		O				D		
S	A	W			Y	E	S	

98. Continents: 1. Europe 2. Asia
3. Africa 4. Australia
Oceans: A. Atlantic B. Pacific C. Indian
100. Cities: 1. Dublin 2. London
3. Moscow 4. Madrid 5. Rome
101.

97.

102.

103.

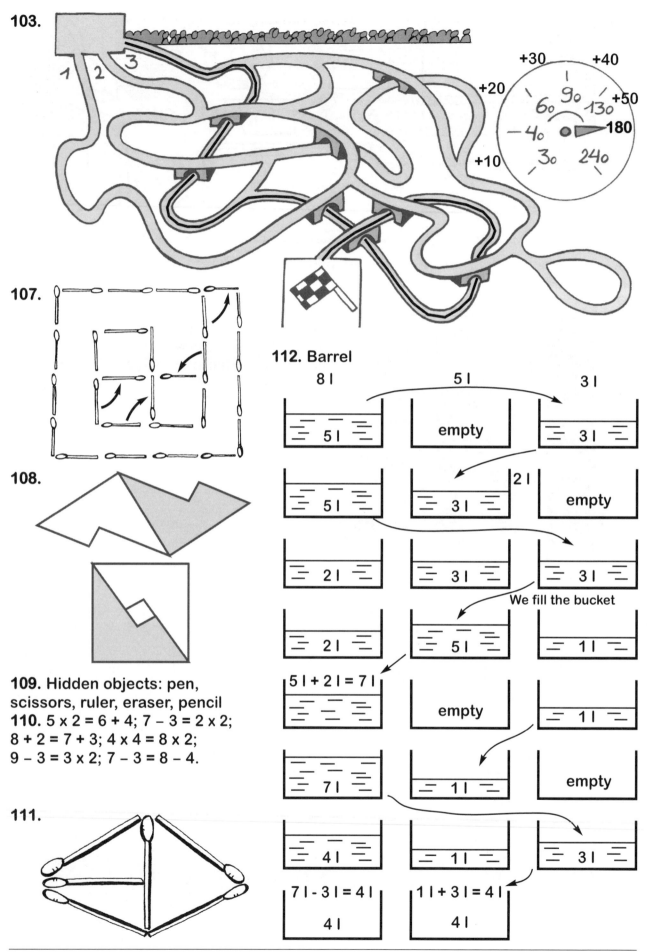

107.

108.

109. Hidden objects: pen, scissors, ruler, eraser, pencil
110. $5 \times 2 = 6 + 4$; $7 - 3 = 2 \times 2$; $8 + 2 = 7 + 3$; $4 \times 4 = 8 \times 2$; $9 - 3 = 3 \times 2$; $7 - 3 = 8 - 4$.

111.

112. Barrel

8 l	5 l	3 l
5 l	empty	3 l
5 l	3 l	empty
2 l	3 l	3 l
2 l	5 l	1 l
$5 l + 2 l = 7 l$	empty	1 l
7 l	1 l	empty
4 l	1 l	3 l
$7 l - 3 l = 4 l$	$1 l + 3 l = 4 l$	
4 l	4 l	

We fill the bucket

113.

114.

115.

116.

117. Symbols:

HIGH VOLTAGE

POISON

RECYCLABLE

RADIOLOGICAL
AGENT

118. Average contents:
$(3 + 4 + 1 + 4 + 2 + 4) \div 6 = 3$

119.

120.

Five of these animals lay eggs: ostrich, condor, crocodile, tortoise, snake
Animals that live in Africa: ostrich, elephant, crocodile, lion, tortoise, snake
Meat eaters: condor, crocodile, lion, snake

121.

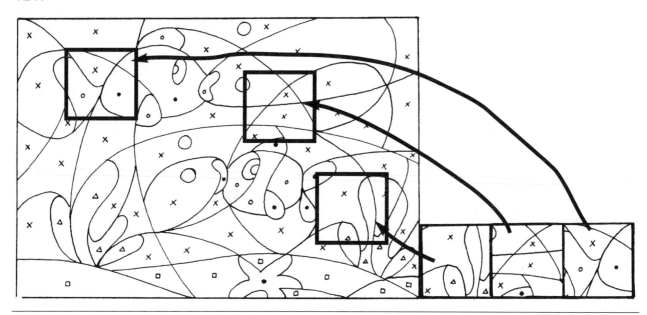

122.

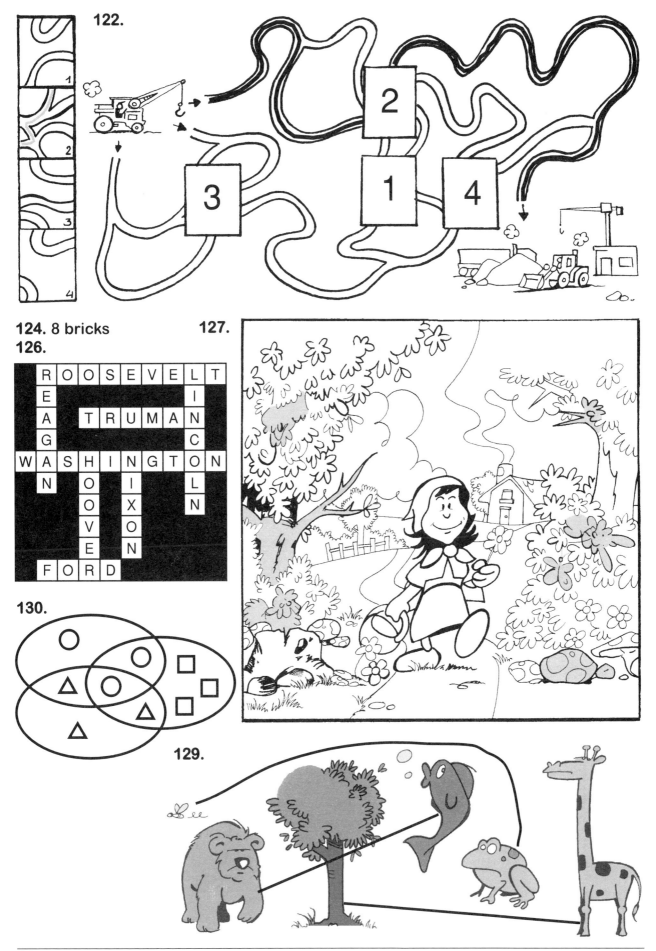

124. 8 bricks

126.

R	O	O	S	E	V	E	L	T	
E								I	
A		T	R	U	M	A	N	C	
G								O	
W	A	S	H	I	N	G	T	O	N
A		O						L	
N		O				I	X	O	N
		V							
		E							
		F	O	R	D				

130.

127.

129.

131.

132.

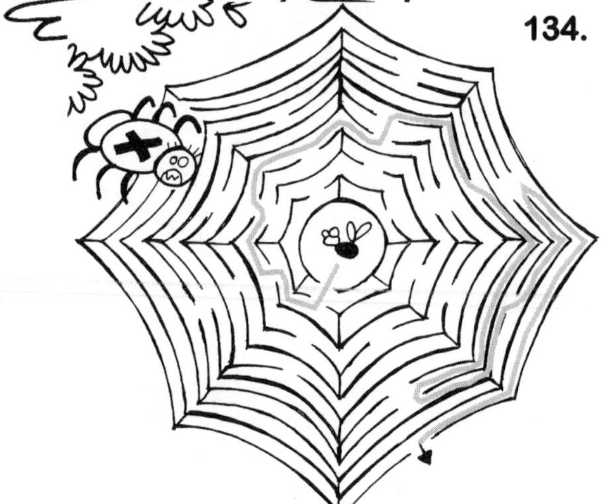

133.

○△ (4 + 21 − 1 = 24)
▭□ (2 × 4 + 23 = 31)
△   (12 − 4 − 4 = 4)
□▭ (33 ÷ 3 + 2 = 13)
▭   (24 ÷ 12 + 1 = 3)

134.

135. In the symbol series, each symbol is made up of a figure and its mirror image. In solving the problems, we will use only the figure (half of the symbol). Therefore, the complete series is:

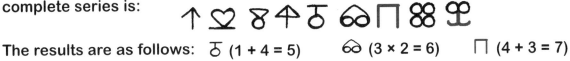

The results are as follows: ॶ (1 + 4 = 5)   ॶ (3 × 2 = 6)   ॶ (4 + 3 = 7)

ॶ (5 – 2 = 3)   ॶ (6 ÷ 3 = 2)   ॶ (4 ÷ 2 = 2)

ॶ (5 – 1 = 4)

137.

1
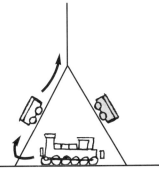

2
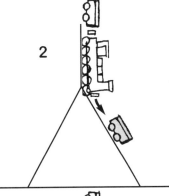

3
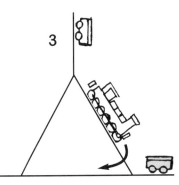

4
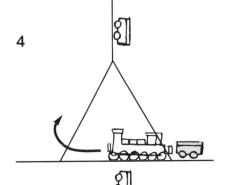

5
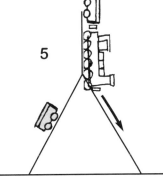

6
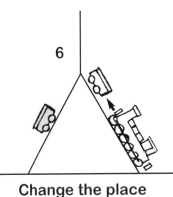

Change the place

7
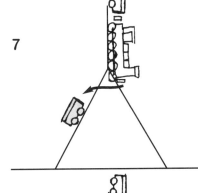

8
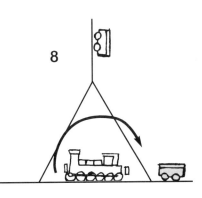

9
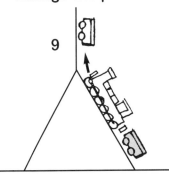

10
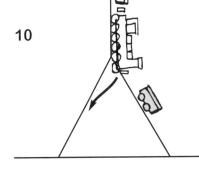

11
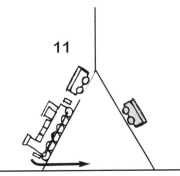

12
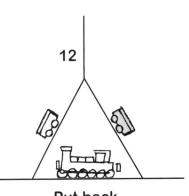

Put back

138. 24 fish

115

139.

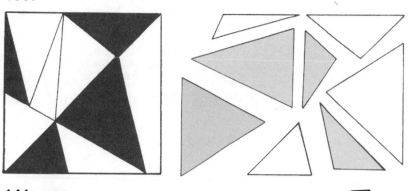

140. Misspelled words (and their correct form): umbrel (umbrella), joging (jogging), hyeroglyph (hieroglyph), imediately (immediately), april (April), masterpice (masterpiece)

142.

2	3	4	5	6
8	1	4	5	12
3	16	3	18	5
4	12	5	12	10
15	3	4	15	18
18	6	12	6	10
9	16	8	10	12

141.

144. 16 leaves.

145. Animals that hibernate: 2, 4

147. Spring: March, April, May; Summer: June, July, August; Fall: September, October, November; Winter: December, January, February

148.

150.

E	N	G	L	A	N	D
R	■	R	L	A	C	E
A	G	O	■	C	W	T
S	U	R	V	E	Y	■
U	■	Y	■	D	O	T
R	A	■	H	E	R	E
E	M	B	A	R	K	■

151. (suggestion)

2	4	3	5	6
3	■	4	■	1
6	0	8	0	6
5	■	1	■	3
4	6	4	2	4

4	5	6	1	4
3	■	2	■	2
8	2	1	1	8
2	■	2	■	2
3	1	9	3	4

152. Misspelled words (and their correct form): hollyday (holiday), helth (health), scisors (scissors), mistery (mystery), spectecles (spectacles), anouncement (announcement), bungallow (bungalow), conztellations (constellations), immagination (imagination), pacefully (peacefully), hypopotamy (hippopotami), costom (custom), buket (bucket), labortory (laboratory)

153.

1	2	3	4	7	8	9	10	11	10	11	14	15	17	18	19	18	17
2	3	4	5	6	8	10	11	12	13	12	13	15	16	17	18	19	18
3	3	4	5	6	7	8	9	10	11	12	13	14	15	16	17	18	17
4	5	6	7	7	10	9	10	11	12	15	16	17	18	19	18		20
5	6	6	7	8	9	10	11	12	13	14	15	16	17	16	15		

154. (3 × 3 + 3) × (3 + 3) = 72, 3 × 3 + 3 × 3 + 3 = 21,
3 × 3 × 3 × 3 - 3 = 78, 3 × 3 × (3 + 3) - 3 = 51,
3 × 3 × 3 - (3 ÷ 3) = 26, (3 + 3 + 3 + 3) × 3 = 36

155. (suggestion)

4	×	6	+	6
×	■		+	■	+
6	+	4	×	6
+	■		×	■	×
6	+	6	×	4

155.

1	2	4	7	11	16	*22*	29	37	46	56	*67*
1	2	3	4	5	6	7	8	9	10	11	

157.

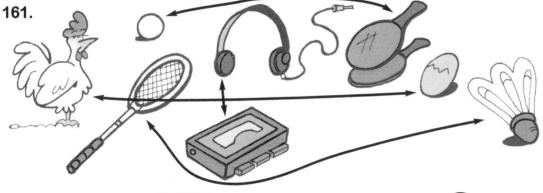

158. 8 instruments: lyre, drum, guitar, recorder, cello, cymbal, sousaphone, bagpipes

161.

162.

163.
(6 × 6 - 6) ÷ 6 = 5
6 + (6 + 6) ÷ 6 = 8
6 + 6 + 6 ÷ 6 = 13
6 × (6 + 6 ÷ 6) = 42
6 × 6 + 6 + 6 = 48
6 × (6 + 6) - 6 = 66
6 × (6 + 6 + 6) = 108
6 × (6 × 6 - 6) = 180

165.

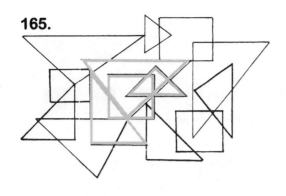

166.

A	B	C	D	E	F	G
1	2	3	4	5	6	7
H	I	J	K	L	M	N
8	9	10	11	12	13	14
O	P	Q	R	S	T	U
15	16	17	18	19	20	21
V	W	X	Y	Z		
22	23	24	25	26		

167. 9696 = 9 + 6 + 9 + 6 = 30 = 3 + 0 = 3
2376 = 2 + 3 + 7 + 6 = 18 = 1 + 8 = 9
5694 = 5 + 6 + 9 + 4 = 24 = 2 + 4 = 6

168.

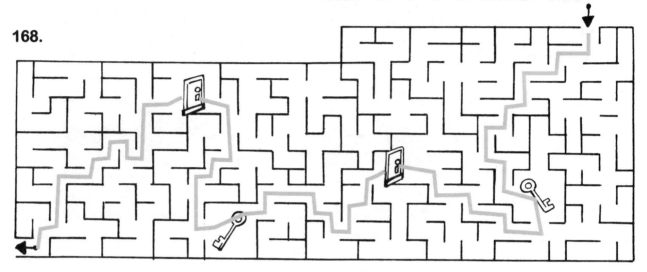

169.

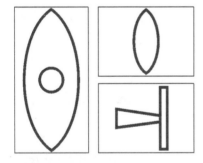

170.

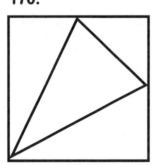

171. shadow # 1.
172.
1. The Olympic Games are held in the leap years.
2. No.
3. The cheetah is the fastest.
4. Six players.
5. Puck.

174. 13 cups.
176. Drinks (suggestion): Punch, Coffee, Lemonade, Milk, Soda, Water
177. $ 23   (21+ 14 + 23 + 8 + 11 = 77; 100 - 77 = 23)
179. 16 shells.
183. Shadows of: 1. electric cel, 2. king-fisher, 3. sawfish, 4. jellyfish
184. Fresh water and sea water animals: 1. piranha, 2. dolphin, 3. octopus, 4. sea horse, 5. whale
185. Tastes: 1. sweet, 2. saltyd, 3. sour

178.

186. Tail fin

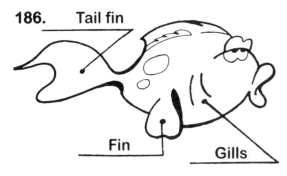

Fin Gills

187. Lock # 3.
188. Stories: 1. Little Red Riding Hood,
2. SnowWhite, 3. The Three Little Pigs,
4. SnowWhite, 5. Tom Thumb
189-190. These instruments are used for
1. hearing the inner sounds of the body,
2. taking the temperature, 3. drinking,
4. throat checking.
Item # 3 doesn't belong here.

192.

193. A. explorer, B. country,
C. Denmark, D. North America,
E. France, F. country

194.

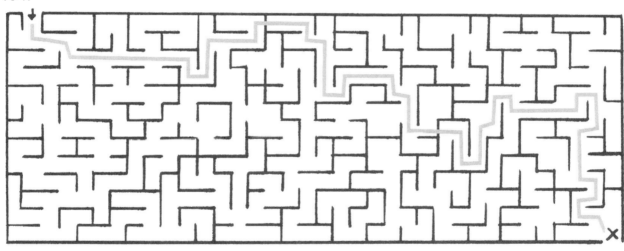

196. Target 87.   **198.**
199. 17 clouds.

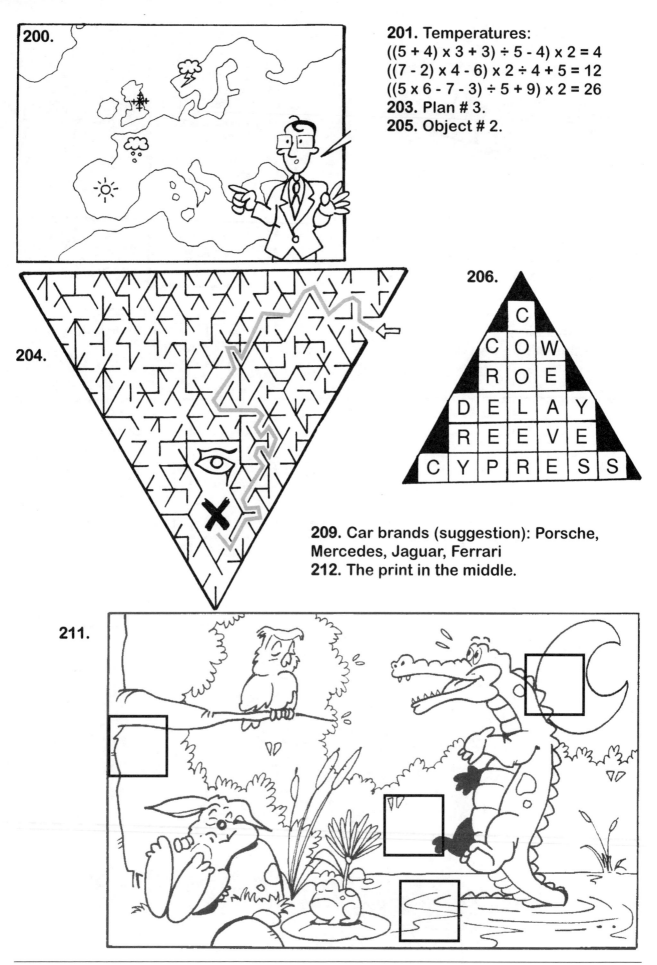

200.

201. Temperatures:
$((5 + 4) \times 3 + 3) \div 5 - 4) \times 2 = 4$
$((7 - 2) \times 4 - 6) \times 2 \div 4 + 5 = 12$
$((5 \times 6 - 7 - 3) \div 5 + 9) \times 2 = 26$
203. Plan # 3.
205. Object # 2.

204.

206.

209. Car brands (suggestion): Porsche, Mercedes, Jaguar, Ferrari
212. The print in the middle.

211.

213.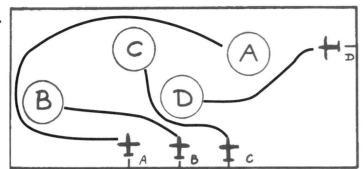

214.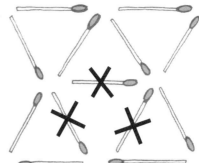

215.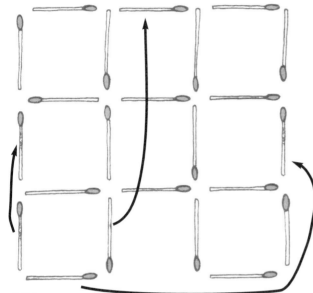

216. Beam # 3.

219.
174 - 42 = 132
180 + 54 = 234
64 x 3 = 192
384 ÷ 2 = 192
288 - 97 = 191

220. Print # 1.

222. Bird # 5 (penguin).
223. The strange animal: rhino horns, horse nostrils, turtle mouth, cow eyes, human hair, elephant ears, gorilla front legs, kangaroo rear legs, lion tail.
224. Shadows of 1. porcupine, 2. owl, 3. snake, 4. rabbit, 5. cat
228. 2 x (4 + 1) = 10, (8 x 2) - 3 = 13, 5 + (9 ÷ 3) = 8, 10 ÷ (5 x 1) = 2, (7 + 4) - 6 = 5, (9 - 6) x 4 = 12

221.

C	O	M	P	U	T	E	R
O	F	I	L	Y	O	C	E
M	I	N	U	S	T	N	S
P	G	U	S	U	A	Q	U
U	U	S	A	M	L	W	L
T	R	W	C	O	U	N	T
E	E	Q	U	A	L	Z	E

230.

231.

233. Shadow # 1 (woman's shoe).
234. Line # 1.
235. Triangle # 2.
236. Two Mexicans riding bikes
237. Four Mexicans playing cards and sitting around a table

238.

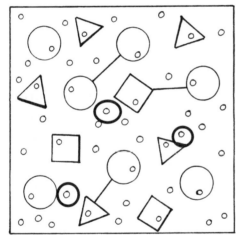 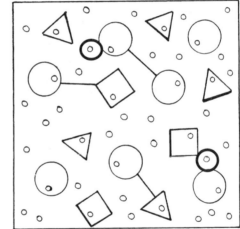

239. Yellow card, red card.

240.

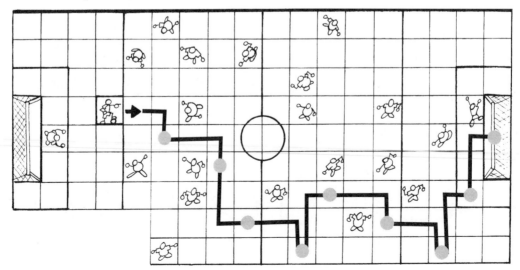

241. Basketball players:
Bryant, Pippen, Iverson, O'Neal, Miller

243. Car brands (suggestion): Ferrari, Chevrolet, Mercedes, Lincoln, Nissan, Audi.

246. Car brands:
1. Mercedes, 2. Ferrari, 3. Dodge, 4. HONDA, 5. BMW

245.

	cars	fruits&vegetable	animals	colors
R	Rolls Royce	Radish	Rhino	Red
B	BMW	Banana	Buffalo	Blue
O	Opel	Orange	Opossum	Orange
P	Pontiac	Peas	Pig	Purple
F	Ford	Fig	Fawn	Fuchsia

247.

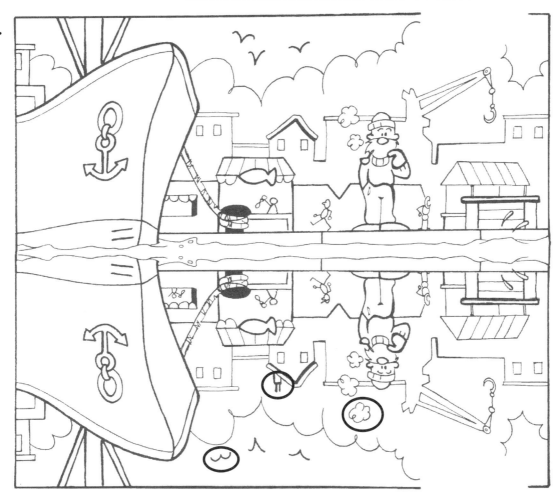

249.

		K		C	O	W	
		I		O			
		W		L			S
	H	K	I	T	T	E	N
	O						A
C	R	A	B	S		F	K
	S		U		M	A	R	E
	E		L			W	
			L	I	O	N	S

250.

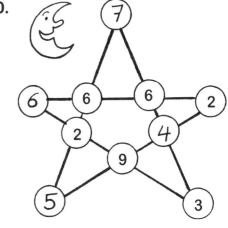

251.

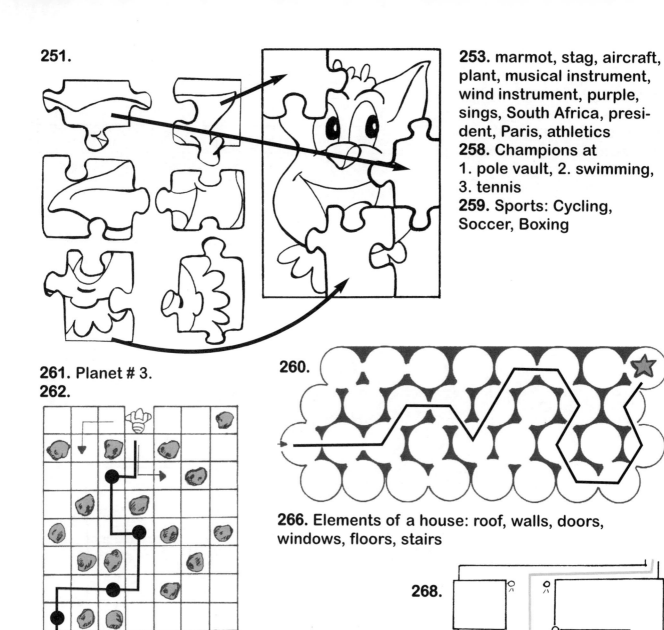

253. marmot, stag, aircraft, plant, musical instrument, wind instrument, purple, sings, South Africa, president, Paris, athletics

258. Champions at
1. pole vault, 2. swimming,
3. tennis

259. Sports: Cycling, Soccer, Boxing

261. Planet # 3.
262.

260.

266. Elements of a house: roof, walls, doors, windows, floors, stairs

268.

267.

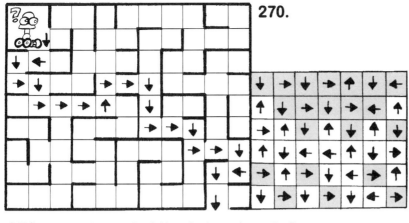

270.

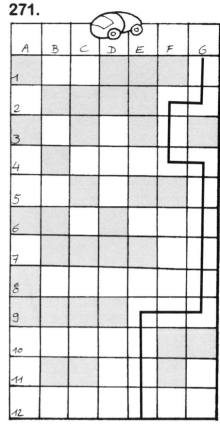

271.

274. Capitals: 1. Dublin, 2. London, 3. Rome,
4. Lisbon, 5. Madrid, 6. Paris, 7. Oslo, 8. Stockholm,
9. Helsinki, 10. Berlin, 11. Bern
275. Continent: Africa
276.

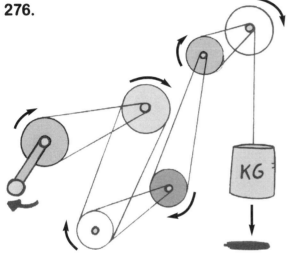

277. Monuments in 1. Belgium, 2. France,
3. Italy
278. Left: 9 packages x 1 lb = 9 lb
Right: 1 package x 5 lb + 2 packages x 2 lb =
= 9 lb
The scales will stay still.

279.

1

2

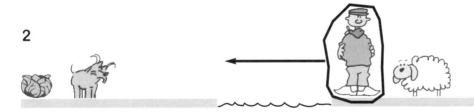

3

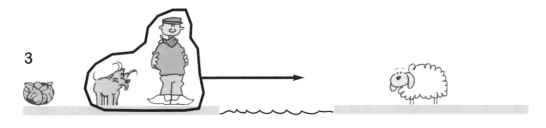

(continued)

4

5

6

7

280.
□ - details
○ - differ-
ences
◇ - mis-
takes

281.

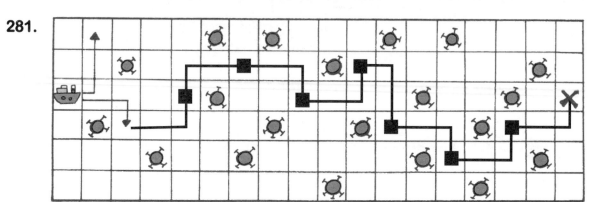

282. 8 = 4 + 4 = 10 - 2 = 64 ÷ 8 = 2 x 4 = 40 ÷ 5 = 24 ÷ 3

284.

283.

287.

	M	A	D		M	A	L	
L	O	N	E		E	V	I	L
I	P		A	W	E		K	O
T	E	A	R		K	N	E	W
		L				E		
B	O	L	D		C	A	L	M
U	P		E	T	A		O	A
M	E	A	N		R	O	S	Y
	N	A	Y			E	S	T

285.

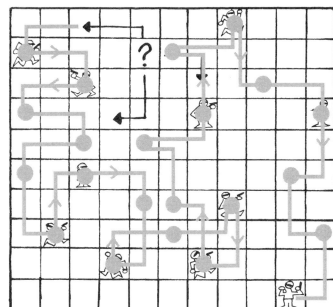

290. ■ will replace the question mark.

294. Animals which give milk: 1, 4

297. I am drinking a glass of milk now.
He doesn't know I'll be fourteen tomorrow.
I wish my mother were here.
Will you be twelve tomorrow?
The teacher tells us to be quiet.

291.

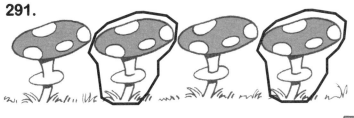

296.

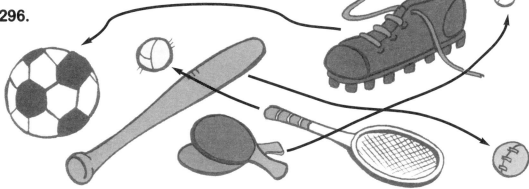

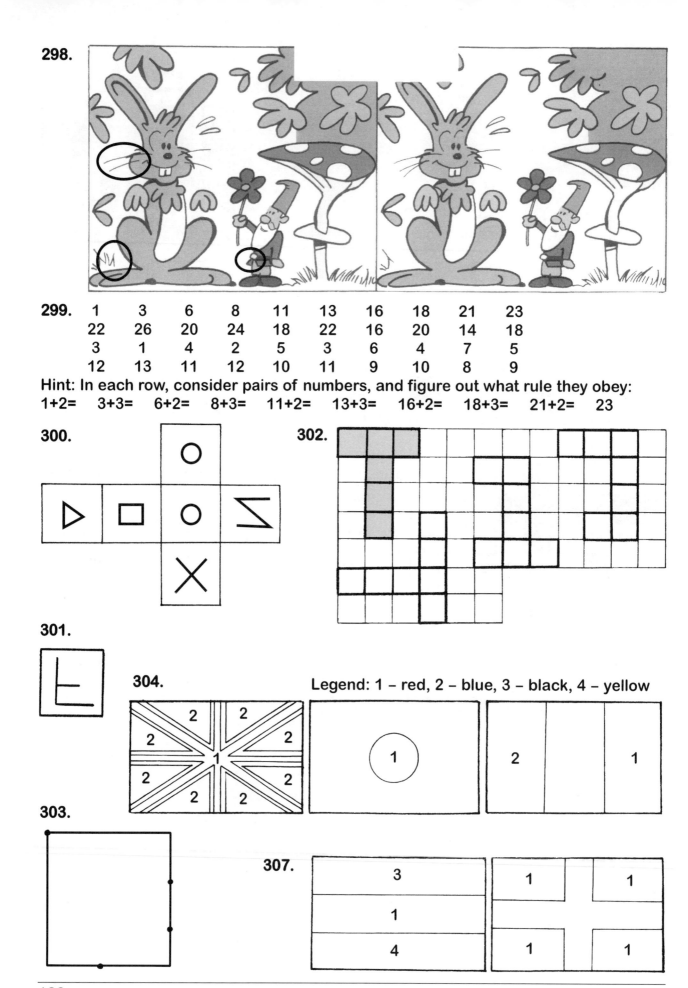

298.

299.

1	3	6	8	11	13	16	18	21	23
22	26	20	24	18	22	16	20	14	18
3	1	4	2	5	3	6	4	7	5
12	13	11	12	10	11	9	10	8	9

Hint: In each row, consider pairs of numbers, and figure out what rule they obey:

1+2=   3+3=   6+2=   8+3=   11+2=   13+3=   16+2=   18+3=   21+2=   23

300.

302.

301.

304.   Legend: 1 – red, 2 – blue, 3 – black, 4 – yellow

303.

307.

128

305-306.

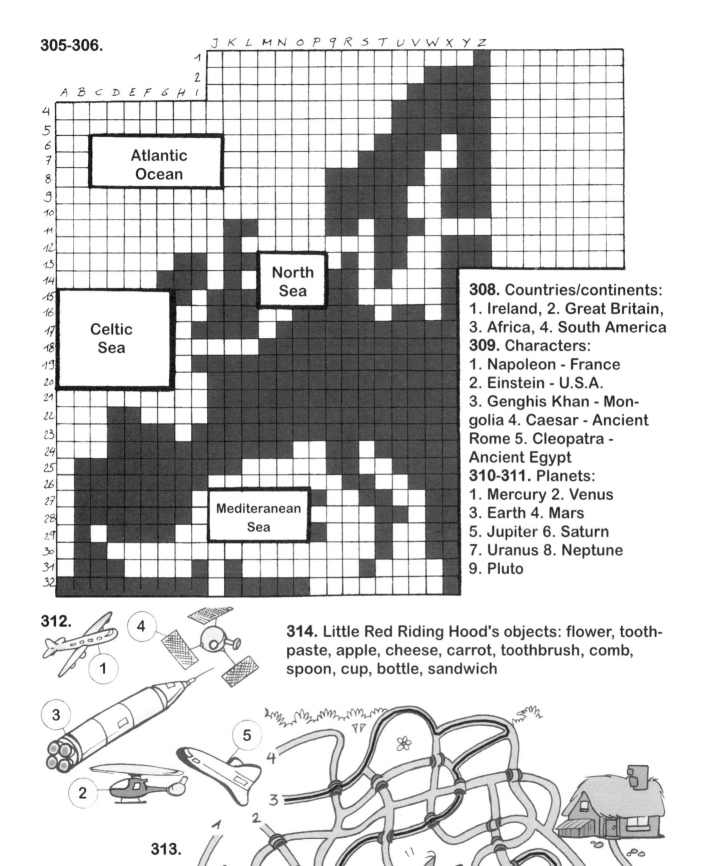

308. Countries/continents:
1. Ireland, 2. Great Britain,
3. Africa, 4. South America
309. Characters:
1. Napoleon - France
2. Einstein - U.S.A.
3. Genghis Khan - Mongolia 4. Caesar - Ancient Rome 5. Cleopatra - Ancient Egypt
310-311. Planets:
1. Mercury 2. Venus
3. Earth 4. Mars
5. Jupiter 6. Saturn
7. Uranus 8. Neptune
9. Pluto

312.

313.

314. Little Red Riding Hood's objects: flower, toothpaste, apple, cheese, carrot, toothbrush, comb, spoon, cup, bottle, sandwich

315.

317.

319. 9 frogs, 10 flowers - fewer frogs than flowers.

322.

323. ▲ will replace the question mark.

320-321.

324.

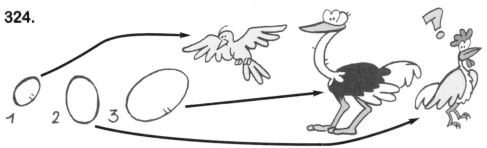

325. Birds: Flamingo, Ostrich, Turkey, Goose

327. One birdhouse.

328. Shadows of 1. parrot, 2. woodpecker, 3. penguin, 4. ostrich, 5. chicken

330. A red-yellow ball.

331.

326.

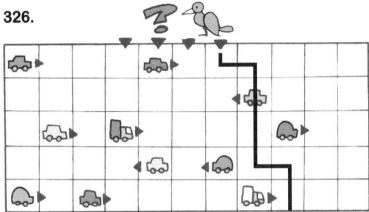

333. Details: whistles, bow tie, giraffe's neck, rhino's horns

335.

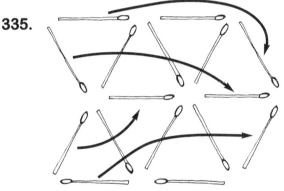

334.

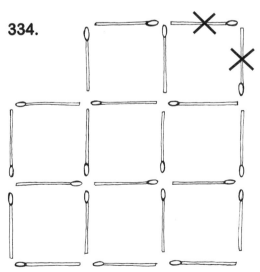

336. 1. Lion, giraffe, rhinoceros, hippopotamus, hyena, gnu (suggestion) 2. Permanently water-logged ground that is usually overgrown and sometimes partly forested 3. Southeast 4. Smell 5. For keeping them safe from floods 6. A monster with a man's head and a lion's body 7. No, it is a mammal, 8. A small passerine songbird 9. Wilbur (1867-1912) and Orville (1871-1948) Wright were US aviation pioneers who designed and flew the first powered aircraft (1903) 10. Giant panda (suggestion) 11. "Sam the Sugar Glider" 12. Life on Earth 13. A system involving the interactions between a community and its non-living environment 14. Africa and India 15. 15 to 173 pairs 16. A famous person who poses for a photographer, or wears clothes and garments to display them to prospective buyers

338.

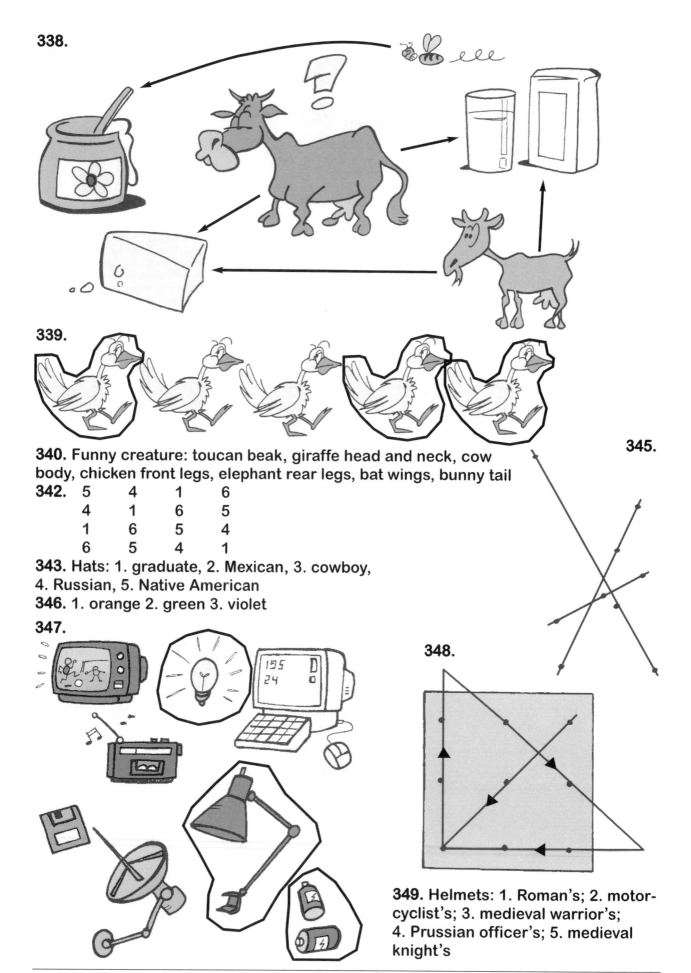

339.

340. Funny creature: toucan beak, giraffe head and neck, cow body, chicken front legs, elephant rear legs, bat wings, bunny tail

342.

5	4	1	6
4	1	6	5
1	6	5	4
6	5	4	1

343. Hats: 1. graduate, 2. Mexican, 3. cowboy, 4. Russian, 5. Native American

346. 1. orange 2. green 3. violet

347.

345.

348.

349. Helmets: 1. Roman's; 2. motor-cyclist's; 3. medieval warrior's; 4. Prussian officer's; 5. medieval knight's

351. $\triangle - \bigcirc = \square$; $\square + \square = \bigcirc$ Hint: We replace $\square = 1$, $\bigcirc = 2$, $\triangle = 3$,
$\bigcirc - \triangle = 3$ Hint: $\triangle + \triangle = 2 \rightarrow \triangle = 1$; $\square - 1 = 4 \rightarrow \square = 5$; $5 - \bigcirc = 1 \rightarrow \bigcirc = 4$.
Therefore $\square = 5$; $\triangle = 1$; $\bigcirc = 4$.

352.

354.

355. Shadows of 1. frog,
2. bird, 3. porcupine,
4. spider
357. The third diamond.

358.

359.

Sunflower   Tulip   Rose

360. Prints of 1.duck,
2. snake, 3. bird,
4. human, 5. bear

361.

362.

363.

1 Songbird with chicks - fly, 2 Mouse - lives on the ground, 3 Spider with baby spiders - live on the ground, 4 Sea bird - flies, 5 Snake - lives on the ground, 6 Fish - lives in the water, 7 Cat with kittens - live on the ground, 8 Fly - flies

364.

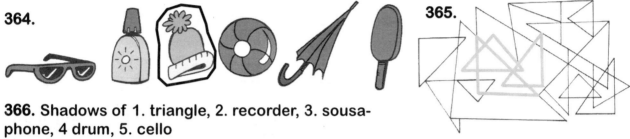

365.

366. Shadows of 1. triangle, 2. recorder, 3. sousaphone, 4 drum, 5. cello

367. Sharp sounds: 1, 2, 5; low sounds: 3, 4

368.

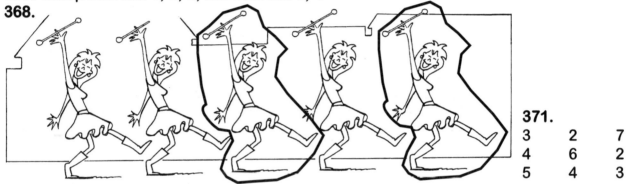

371.

3	2	7
4	6	2
5	4	3

372. YELLOWSTONE

373. 7 x 10 - 2 - 4 = 64; 2 x 10 = 20; 7 + 4 = 11; 4 x 25 - 10 - 2 - 7 + 5 = 86; 10 x 25 - 7 x 2 - 5 = 231

374.

S	D	P	I	G	W	O	L	F	B	E	A	R
C	M	E	T	O	G	N	U	T	E	M	B	C
S	A	L	M	O	N	A	O	U	A	O	A	O
H	G	I	S	P	S	C	R	V	N	D	C	
E	P	C	R	E	B	O	A	K	E	K	G	K
E	A	N	T	E	A	T	I	E	R	E	E	F
P	E	N	F	O	X	S	Q	Y	O	R	A	
L	I	Z	A	R	D	S	H	O	R	S	E	W
O	P	A	R	T	R	I	D	G	E	H	E	N

377.

379. Hint:
The red boat - 9 jumps
The green boat - 8 jumps
The yellow boat - 8 jumps
The blue boat - 7 jumps
The blue boat is the winner.

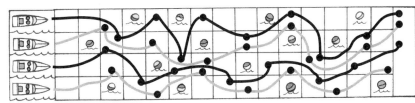

381.

380.

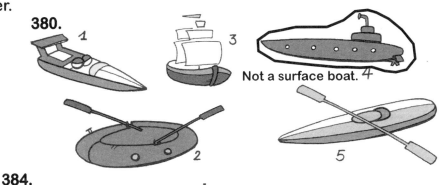

Not a surface boat.

382. Boot # 3.
383. The 2nd guy's shadow.

384.

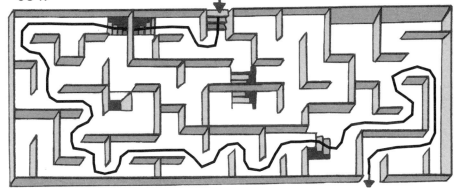

385. Famous detectives (suggestion):
1. Sherlock Holmes
2. Hercule Poirot
3. Philip Marlowe
4. Miss Marple

386. Shadows of
1. airplane, 2. bicycle,
3. jet boat, 4. car,
5. zeppelin

387. The bicycle doesn't belong to the series as it doesn't have an engine.

388.

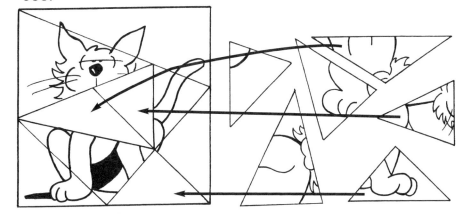

389-390.

391.

392. Fragment # 2.

393.

9	3	5
1	4	7
8	6	2

394. Answers: painter, animal, dwelling, writer, South Pole, Egypt, snake, mammal, man, jar, plant, man

395. 100 peas.

396. Pumpkin, bottles, matchbox, mice.

397.

398. The shadow in the middle.

399.

400. You can find the answer between the choices written below each calculation.